THE HAUNTING OF ROSE ABBEY

The Arrogant Earls Novella

Kathleen Ayers

© Copyright 2023 by Kathleen Ayers
Text by Kathleen Ayers
Cover by Dar Albert

Dragonblade Publishing, Inc. is an imprint of Kathryn Le Veque Novels, Inc.
P.O. Box 23
Moreno Valley, CA 92556
ceo@dragonbladepublishing.com

Produced in the United States of America

First Edition September 2023
Print Edition

Reproduction of any kind except where it pertains to short quotes in relation to advertising or promotion is strictly prohibited.

All Rights Reserved.

The characters and events portrayed in this book are fictitious. Any similarity to real persons, living or dead, is purely coincidental and not intended by the author.

ARE YOU SIGNED UP FOR DRAGONBLADE'S BLOG?

You'll get the latest news and information on exclusive giveaways, exclusive excerpts, coming releases, sales, free books, cover reveals and more.

Check out our complete list of authors, too!

No spam, no junk. That's a promise!

Sign Up Here

www.dragonbladepublishing.com

Dearest Reader;

Thank you for your support of a small press. At Dragonblade Publishing, we strive to bring you the highest quality Historical Romance from some of the best authors in the business. Without your support, there is no 'us', so we sincerely hope you adore these stories and find some new favorite authors along the way.

Happy Reading!

CEO, Dragonblade Publishing

Additional Dragonblade books by Author Kathleen Ayers

The Five Deadly Sins Series
Sinfully Wed (Book 1)
Sinfully Tempted (Book 2)

The Arrogant Earls Series
Forgetting the Earl (Book 1)
Chasing the Earl (Book 2)
Enticing the Earl (Book 3)
The Haunting of Rose Abbey (Novella)

Chapter One

"You're Collins?"

Miss Edwina Collins clasped her hands before her and took in the imposing gentleman behind the desk. "I am, Lord Bascomb."

She brushed away a strand of her hair stuck to her cheek. The smells of her traveling clothes, wet wool, and dirt filled her nostrils. Mud clung to the hem of her skirts. The trip to this remote estate a stone's throw away from the Scottish border had not been achieved without some difficulty. She was not at her best.

"The Collins I hired to serve as my secretary?" A snort. "You are supposed to be male."

Under normal circumstances, when she didn't look like a bedraggled rat, Edwina's usual rigid politeness would come to the forefront and serve her well in dealing with Lord Bascomb. She'd known him less than an hour and already found him to be the rudest human being she'd ever encountered.

"As you can see, I am not. Nonetheless, you extended an offer of employment and I accepted," she said in a tart, no-nonsense tone.

Bascomb had massive shoulders. Big hands. Edwina supposed if he had bothered to stand when she entered the study, he would tower over her by at least a foot or more. He narrowed his eyes at her, an arresting combination of grayish green, the same hue as the lichen-strewn boulders bordering the hole-ridden road up from Portsmith where the coach had dropped her. She'd counted the immense boulders on the journey while clinging to the edge of the pony cart as it labored up the hill to Rose Abbey.

"And your cousin is the Earl of Southwell?" Bascomb possessed a rather wicked-looking scar, which neatly divided the left side of his face. The puckered flesh snaked from the corner of his eye down to the edge of his lip.

His very full bottom lip. Oddly sensual for such a boorish man.

What a thing to notice at the moment, Edwina.

"Lord Southwell is indeed my cousin."

Edwina wasn't about to add that South had written the recommendation for his spinster cousin under duress. Or that he was now halfway to Egypt with his new bride and unavailable to answer any more of Lord Bascomb's irritating questions. All she'd asked of South was that the recommendation make no mention of her sex so that she might secure a position based on her abilities. She may also have asked him to accidentally omit the 'a' after her name, which had given Bascomb the impression she was Edwin and not Edwina. A small mistake that may have continued throughout her correspondence with Bascomb. It was no one's fault really.

"I'm happy to know the truth was not stretched on that pertinent fact," he growled from behind the desk. "But I seem to recall the recommendation was for *Edwin* Collins."

Bascomb, or any gentleman, was unlikely to hire a woman. The salary he offered was far more than what a lady's companion or governess could earn, two positions Edwina was not remotely suitable for. She was, however, quite capable at ledgers, correspondence, and organization.

"I cannot speak for Lord Southwell, but mistakes happen. I'm sure it was merely an oversight."

"Which you allowed to continue."

Edwina cleared her throat. Really, wouldn't it be polite if Bascomb asked her to sit instead of continuing to allow her to stand before him with mud dripping off her skirts? "My skills are exemplary, my lord."

"You've wasted your time in coming here, Collins," Bascomb snarled, sounding very much like the grumpy, elderly curmudgeon Edwina had pictured him to be. During their short correspondence, she had the impression he was an older gentleman. Gray-haired, of course. Perhaps slightly addled. Bascomb admitted to her in his letters that he'd had enormous trouble keeping a secretary. She'd wrongly assumed his failure in keeping the position filled was due to the remote location of Rose Abbey.

Now Edwina had a suspicion the cause was Bascomb's personality. Or lack thereof.

"You don't seem to be in a position to be picky," she replied. "Or have you another candidate?"

A second growl came from Bascomb. His eyes traveled over her bedraggled form dressed in the damp wool, frowning as a small clod of dirt fell with a plop from the edge of her hem.

"And I'm *here*." Edwina bristled under his assessment. "Ready to take on the task of organizing your affairs."

"Prickly, aren't you, Collins?" There was just the tiniest glint of amusement in those unusual eyes.

"It has been a long journey." Edwina had been jostled across half of England for two full days. Trapped with strangers in a coach, none of whom believed in the most basic principles of hygiene. She'd gasped for air at every stop. She was tired. Hungry. Dirty. And she hadn't come all this way to have Bascomb turn her out without at least giving her a chance to prove herself.

"I should send you back to Portsmith so you can return you from whence you came. Outside London somewhere, I assume." Bascomb waved a large hand.

Edwina looked out the window as thunder rattled the ancient panes of glass, and waited. She stretched her fingers, bruised from clutching the seat of the pony cart. "Hampshire," she answered. Bascomb knew perfectly well where she'd traveled from. He'd sent her the money for the journey here.

Bascomb shrugged his pair of mountainous shoulders as if Hampshire and the environs of London were one and the same. The green-gray gaze flicked over her, settling somewhere in the region of her bosom, before returning to her face.

A small sensation of heat curled down the length of Edwina's body. A wholly unexpected reaction and one that made her unsure if she'd done the right thing in coming to Rose Abbey.

Rose Abbey—once a haven for a group of Benedictine nuns, when convents and monasteries dotted England—was a dark, imposing place. The estate lay at the very end of a long road, all uphill, through woods so dense little sunlight filtered through the trees. Midway up the rise of the hill, Edwina had thought night had fallen. Her first sight of Rose Abbey had not reassured her.

The part of the estate that had once been the abbey erupted out of the ground just outside the study window. A series of wide gothic arches stretched up toward the sky, like the skeleton of some huge, forgotten creature whose bones had been picked clean. Roses were everywhere, crawling up the house as if to tear the stone apart. The bushes sprung from the ruins in wild disarray. Crimson blooms sprouted from the sprawling bramble of thorns. Not a hint of pink, white, or any other color. It gave the illusion Rose Abbey was dripping blood.

Most disturbing and not the least welcoming.

The wind flung an untrimmed mass of twisting, torn buds against the window, the thorns scratching along the glass with an eerie sound, making Edwina's teeth rattle. The house shuddered as rain lashed against the panes.

"I won't send you back to Hampshire tonight," Bascomb said in a grim tone. "Not in this weather."

"How very kind of you." Edwina turned back from the window to observe him once more. Her skin tingled, the earlier warmth from his regard still lingering over her skin. The moment she'd been ushered into the study and caught sight of the large male sitting behind the desk, a shiver had cascaded down the length of her arms. At first, Edwina had thought it only the chill of the day, of the horrible rasping from the rosebushes as they clawed at the house.

But it was Bascomb.

The last time Edwina's body had hummed in the presence of a man was years ago. Just before her family had fallen into genteel poverty and her hopes of wedding without a dowry had disappeared. Now, at the age of twenty-nine, Edwina was an avowed spinster. Such feelings as Bascomb now aroused had been firmly pushed to the back of her mind. Locked away. Examined only late at night when Edwina was alone in her bed.

Such instant...*arousal* for Bascomb was frankly more unsettling than Rose Abbey itself.

He wasn't even handsome, at least in the conventional sense. His features were savagely hewn. Those glowing green-gray eyes, far too beautiful to belong to a man, were set atop bold slashes of cheekbones. Inky black hair, straight and thick, fell to brush the tops of his broad shoulders. No cravat. No coat. Waistcoat hanging open. His shirt unbuttoned enough to give a glimpse of lightly tanned skin at his throat.

Edwina shivered again.

His entire appearance, including the wicked scar stretching down the left side of his face, gave Bascomb the look of a pirate. All he was lacking was an eye patch and a parrot perched on his shoulder.

She looked down at her poor, battered half boots. Bascomb possessed a potent, striking masculinity. Few women would be immune to him. Edwina certainly wasn't. Resolutely, she pushed such thoughts aside and lifted her gaze to his once more.

Lightning flashed outside the window, throwing the ruins of the abbey and abandoned church with its collection of gravestones into stark relief. Thunder shook the windowpanes once more.

Bascomb muttered a string of curses under his breath. Most had to do with Edwina. None were the least polite, and the last few caused her cheeks to pink slightly. She was no prude. She hadn't been a maid in many years, but...well, *good Lord.*

"My lord." She gave him an unflinching look, determined to brave this out despite her attraction to Bascomb, and his attempts to intimidate her. "Did you not state your need for a secretary? Someone who could organize your affairs, handle the ledgers, and reply to correspondence? Despite my—" Edwina searched for the proper word.

"Femaleness?"

"Yes. That." She clasped her fingers tighter. "The polite thing to do would be to at least allow me the opportunity to show you how I can be of assistance." There was a plea hidden in her words, the desperation seeping through her show of bravery no matter how hard she struggled to keep it at bay. If Bascomb turned her away, Edwina wasn't sure what she would do.

"What about me, *Collins*, strikes you as the least polite?" Massive fingers drummed atop the desk. Thick. Blunt. How would they feel tugging at the buttons of her dress? Or possibly searching beneath her skirts?

Good Lord. Something is terribly wrong with me.

"Did anyone mention to you," Bascomb grumbled, "why I've run through almost every earnest *male* secretary in England? Why I've had so much difficulty, *Collins*?" There was a tiny, almost invisible tug at his lips. The puckered skin bisecting his left cheek danced.

Wretch. He's enjoying my discomfort.

Edwina straightened her shoulders. "I assume their rapid departures have something to do with your charming personality, my lord," she snapped. The impolite response was the result of her wet clothes, growling stomach, and unexpected attraction to Bascomb. It was certainly not the load of tripe that McDeaver, the owner of the pony cart that had transported her here, had filled her ears with during their blessedly brief acquaintance.

Something like approval gleamed in Bascomb's eyes at her sharp retort. "I'm sure McDeaver took great pleasure informing you of what to expect upon your arrival."

"From you, my lord? Or Rose Abbey?"

McDeaver *had* taken morbid delight in relaying the gruesome tale of Rose Abbey. As had the wife of the tavern owner who'd brought Edwina tea while she'd waited for McDeaver to be located. And one of the laborers at the table next to Edwina had seen fit to embellish the tale and give his opinion. The denizens of Portsmith had eyed Edwina with pity while she'd bitten into the stale biscuits served with her tea, whispering about the terrors that awaited her at Rose Abbey.

Haunted. Cursed. Someone may have even said the abbey stood at the gates to hell.

Bascomb's beautiful eyes roved over Edwina once more. It appeared his interest was not solely related to whether she could organize his correspondence properly.

Another burst of heat stretched out across her limbs.

"You've got spine, Collins. I grant you that."

"So I've been told." The trait, while useful when dealing with a rude gentleman she must compel to keep her on as his secretary, made Edwina an unsuitable candidate for marriage. Her lack of a proper dowry didn't help. Passably pretty looks combined with a sharp tongue weren't enough to sway any gentleman to wed her without something more for their trouble.

"Mr. Fielding"—Bascomb's paw of a hand stretched across the desk as if reaching for her—"bolted from Rose Abbey in the middle of the night, wearing nothing more than a nightshirt for his sprint down the hill to Portsmith. Boniest knees I've ever seen on a man. The idiot is fortunate he didn't trip on the way down the road in the dark and break his neck."

"Mr. Fielding?" Edwina asked.

"Your predecessor. He refused to return to collect his things. I had to send them on to Portsmith at great expense to myself."

There was a vengeful spirit roaming the estate, at least according to McDeaver. The specter of the final abbess who presided here. She hadn't left Rose Abbey quietly, sacrificing herself and the group of nuns who'd lived here. The abbess had refused to accept the rule of her sovereign, claiming she only answered to God. The nuns had been raped and slaughtered, the abbess run through with a sword. Whatever wealth the abbey had possessed was never found. The abbess, McDeaver insisted, still haunted Rose Abbey to this day.

Absolutely ridiculous.

"Perhaps Mr. Fielding had a delicate constitution," she replied. "I, however, do not."

Edwina didn't believe in ghosts. Nor vengeful nuns. The exodus from Rose Abbey was more likely the result of Bascomb being a difficult master. She had pointed out to McDeaver, during his macabre recitation of the butchering of innocent nuns, that there was a staff in place at Rose Abbey. Surely if the abbey was haunted, it would be difficult for Lord Bascomb to keep servants as well.

McDeaver had shot her a churlish look.

When the pony cart had pulled up in front of Rose Abbey, a maid had promptly opened the weathered doors and greeted Edwina. True, the girl was somewhat timid. Pale. Her voice had trembled as she'd introduced herself as Meg.

Edwina's trunks had been unceremoniously launched out of the pony cart to land in the dirt. McDeaver had snapped the reins and started back down the road toward Portsmith without so much as a goodbye.

"Could it be possible Mr. Fielding found the working conditions not to his liking?" she said rather pointedly to Bascomb.

Bascomb's lips twitched once more. "I can't imagine, Collins."

More rain pelted the windows. The fireplace hissed as dripping moisture found its way down the chimney. Finally, Bascomb gave a sigh of resignation, apparently coming to some sort of decision. He shoved a messy stack of papers toward her. "There is a desk set up in the library for your use. Perhaps you can sort through these tonight in return for a bed and a warm meal."

Edwina schooled her features, careful not to let the triumph show in her face. Bascomb could bluster all he liked, but it was clear he needed help. A great deal of it. Ledgers were strewn all over the study, as well as papers, inkwells, bits of string, and what looked like a stuffed ferret. "I would be happy to, my lord."

"But I'm sending you back to Portsmith tomorrow once the weather clears," he groused. "Don't bother to unpack."

"I understand completely, my lord." Edwina picked up the stack of papers. She would have preferred to be allowed to change and wash the dirt from her hands and face before starting such a monumental task, but the fact remained Bascomb wasn't tossing her out. At least not yet. "Where would I find the library, my lord?"

"Go back to the staircase and then down the hall on the other side." His attention returned to his desk, pencil flying across a piece of paper. She tried to catch a glimpse of what he was sketching, but all she could make out was the shape of a peaked roof.

Edwina came forward and picked up the stack of papers at the edge of his desk. Struggling with her wet skirts and the correspondence, she made her way out of the study. Rain battered the house as the wind howled around the stone. She could almost make out the sound of the waves crashing violently against the cliffs outside. The hill Rose Abbey sat atop ended with massive, unscalable cliffs above the ocean. Purposefully, Edwina knew, to avoid Viking raiders who had once plied the coast. Rose Abbey's isolation had allowed the nuns who lived here to flourish, forgotten by the rest of the world for hundreds of years.

Until someone had remembered and their peaceful existence had ended.

Chapter Two

EXHAUSTION SEEPED INTO Edwina's bones as she made her way out of the study. Perhaps it was her fatigue that accounted for the heaviness settling about her shoulders. Or the sadness that suddenly filled her.

Damn McDeaver and his lurid tales.

After marching back to the staircase leading to the second floor, she turned to head down the opposite side of the house and caught sight of her trunk sitting in the foyer. A woman stood before the battered trunk, dressed all in black with a lace cap perched atop her gray-streaked hair. Painfully thin to the point of gauntness, the woman was all sharp bones and angles. A sour expression hovered about her lips, the woman evidently not the least pleased at the sight of Edwina. Or possibly it was the muddy trail Edwina was leaving across the floor.

"I am Mrs. Page," the woman announced without preamble, her voice as sharp as the rest of her. "Lord Bascomb's housekeeper. I'll have your things"—she cast a withering stare at Edwina's trunk—"taken upstairs. A room has been prepared for you."

"Thank you, Mrs. Page. I am Miss Collins. Lord Bascomb's secretary."

"Indeed." A brow raised at Edwina. Mrs. Page had eyes like bits of jet, flinty and hard, with little interest in Edwina other than annoyance. "I see he wishes you to go to work immediately." She nodded to the papers clutched in Edwina's arms. "Not unexpected. Mr. Fielding left quite a mess in his haste to escape Rose Abbey. Please follow me and I'll escort you to the library."

"There isn't a parlor or—"

"All His Lordship's secretaries work in the library." She shook her head. "Much to their displeasure. Follow me, Miss Collins." Her skirts rustled softly as she set out down the hall to the left of the stairs. "This portion of Rose Abbey is original." She gestured with one hand. "And was once the residence of the abbess. This wing is smaller, with fewer rooms, but it does contain the library, which was once the private quarters and office of the abbess. When the first Lord Bascomb took ownership of the property, he chose to build around her original home instead of tearing it down or allowing the stone to fall to rubble as he did to the remainder of the abbey and the church. That first Lord Bascomb was not a religious gentleman."

"I saw the ruins outside Lord Bascomb's study."

"The entire backs of both wings face what remains of the original structure. Lord Bascomb's study is directly opposite the library but on the other side. The entire west wing was added in increments by each succeeding Bascomb."

"I see." The slight difference in architecture as they moved into the older part of the house became readily apparent. The wood-paneled walls gave way to stone. The ceilings were lower, the space of the hall tighter. Mildly claustrophobic. Edwina had the strange sensation Rose Abbey was trying to swallow her.

Mrs. Page stopped, swinging open two large double doors at the end of the hall. "I expected His Lordship might have you begin your work today and lit the fire in anticipation. The stone walls keep this part of the house chilly and damp. Your quarters will feel much the same way." She looked up at the ceiling. "They are directly above this room. Closer to the library for your convenience."

"Thank you."

Edwina stepped into the library, taking in the room before her.

The octagon shape of the library was unexpected, as were the high, arched windows at the back that gave a clear view of the abandoned church and the cliffs beyond. An enormous fireplace took up the entire right wall, the stone crumbling in places, and the flames licked and hissed, devouring a stack of logs. Probably original to this part of the house. Above the fireplace hung a portrait of a woman dressed in flowing dark robes. A white headdress completely covered her hair and part of her forehead.

"Lady Renalda," Mrs. Page said in a solemn tone. "The final abbess. This was her office."

Of course it was.

Edwina looked up at the stern, unsmiling woman. McDeaver and the residents of Portsmith reviled the abbess for sacrificing her flock for the sake of her own stubborn pride. The woman in the portrait was younger than Edwina had expected. And pretty. A small bouquet of roses lay in her lap, crimson like all the roses Edwina had seen thus far. Piercing blue eyes gazed back at Edwina, seeming to follow her progress toward the small desk beside the fireplace.

Lady Renalda certainly had the look of a vengeful spirit.

"I'll have Meg bring you tea and something to eat, Miss Collins. I believe you'll find ink and paper in the desk."

"Thank you, Mrs. Page. Tea would be most welcome."

Edwina waited until the housekeeper left before settling herself at the desk. Her head fell to the wooden surface as she tried to pull back the wave of trepidation filling her. If she were wise, Edwina would head back to Portsmith as soon as the rain stopped. Her cousin, Southwell, had offered Edwina a home at his country estate. She could stay as long as she liked. Organize all the artifacts he'd collected on his travels.

Looking around at the coldness surrounding her, Edwina thought maybe she should have taken South's kind offer. But then, as now, Edwina couldn't imagine living on her cousin's charity for the remainder of her days. She had no desire to be the poor, forgotten spinster relation who was trotted out at family gatherings only to be viewed with pity. The very idea made Edwina feel small and insignificant.

Edwina lifted her head. She must brave this out. It was far too late for second thoughts. She was here. The correspondence before her was an excellent start to prove her worth to Bascomb before moving on to the ledgers. Not only was her penmanship splendid, but Edwina's attention to detail, along with her love of numbers, was a singular skill. Her ability allowed her to spot errors others did not, particularly useful when keeping her father's books.

A sudden wash of sadness pierced Edwina's chest. Her father had tried desperately to hide the truth of their approaching poverty, but Edwina had seen how the ledgers had been padded just the same. She'd done what she could, stretching every shilling to ensure there would be coal and something to eat in the larder. Kept a roof over their heads for far longer than anyone thought possible. In the end, all her efforts hadn't mattered. She'd still been forced to sell everything.

Edwina craned her neck to the side and caught Lady Renalda glaring at her with those judgmental eyes. Why did Bascomb keep the portrait of the abbess? Seemed odd given Lady Renalda's reputation for haunting.

Lightning streaked across the windows at the back of the library, followed by another roar of thunder.

Two very distinct thuds came from the bookcase nearest the windows, along with the sound of something moving along the floor.

Edwina leaned back in the chair, peering into the gloom. The library could benefit from better lighting. The back of her neck prickled, and she had the sense she was not alone in the room. Her pulse fluttered unsteadily, fear clogging her throat.

She cursed McDeaver again for filling her head with nonsense.

Pushing back from the desk, Edwina stood, clutching the pen before her like a weapon.

"Hello?"

Moving silently toward the other side of the library, Edwina made her way to the row of bookcases and peeked around the corner. Two books lay sprawled, spines up, on the floor. Lowering the pen and feeling like an idiot, she marched over and picked up both tomes. Sliding both books back into the empty spot on the bookshelf, she took a deep breath, willing her pulse to slow.

"Nothing but thunder," she said out loud. "The vibrations from the storm shook the house, which in turn rattled the bookshelves, causing the books to fall to the floor." A laugh came from her. "Nothing ghostly about it. When next I see Mr. McDeaver, I shall have a word with him about filling me with tales of a crazed abbess haunting Rose Abbey. If I—"

The words stalled in her mouth as another thump sounded from the other side of the library. The bookcases there nearly reached the ceiling, sitting flush against the wall. She pushed her hands into her skirts to stop the slight tremble of her fingers, nearly dropping the pen. There was nothing amiss. No books on the floor. Nothing out of place.

Feeling foolish and instructing her imagination to rein itself in, she marched back to the center of the room, stopping before the portrait of the abbess.

"I don't believe in you," Edwina whispered.

"Miss?"

Edwina gasped, her hand coming to her throat before she turned and saw Meg in the doorway.

Good Lord. She'd not even been here an entire day and already she was imagining things. She was not a woman who was easily startled. Or even fanciful. The house was old. The bookcases looked quite ancient. She'd be lucky if they didn't suddenly burst apart and all come tumbling down upon her while she worked.

A large tray was held aloft in Meg's quivering hands. "I've brought your tea, Miss Collins." Her eyes darted to the portrait of the abbess before fixing back on Edwina, features stamped with fear. The tea tray trembled, the cup clattering against the saucer.

"Hello, Meg." Waving her away from the desk, Edwina instead directed Meg to set down the tray on a low table next to an overstuffed settee. "Please place the tray there. It looks quite heavy." Laden with tea and a vast assortment of sandwiches and pastries, the tray tilted as the maid struggled to place it on the table. Edwina's stomach grumbled. She hadn't thought Mrs. Page would be so generous based on their initial introduction. "My goodness, I must appear to be incredibly hungry."

Meg took a shaky breath as she set down the tray, looking once more at the portrait of Lady Renalda. "Yes, Miss Collins." She bobbed. "Mrs. Page said Lord Bascomb may join you so Cook made sure to include extra. No watercress or cucumber. His Lordship don't like a tea tray that ain't hearty."

So there was *also* a cook at Rose Abbey. Plus Mrs. Page and Meg. And a footman or possibly a butler. The housekeeper didn't look strong enough to carry Edwina's trunk upstairs herself.

"Hearty?" Edwina smiled at the maid, who was obviously uncomfortable at being in the library.

"There's roast beef and ham." Meg nodded at the tray. "Roast beef is His Lordship's favorite."

"I'll be sure to concentrate on the ham," Edwina assured the maid.

Meg gave her a weak smile and exited the library by backing out, her eyes never leaving the portrait of Lady Renalda, as if the abbess would jump out of the portrait and grab her.

Once she was alone again, Edwina's gaze went to the other side of the library, where the second thump had come from. She strolled along the wall of bookcases, taking note of the sheer volume of tomes and their dusty condition. If there was something out of place, Edwina couldn't tell.

I'm being ridiculous.

Her stomach rumbled again, so Edwina went back to the tray and poured herself a steaming cup of tea. She filled a plate, taking care to include roast beef purely because it was sure to irritate Bascomb, and sat at the desk. Edwina sipped at her tea, ate two sandwiches, and felt better immediately. She'd only been hungry. Tired. A cup of tea and something in her stomach made a world of difference.

Thus fortified, Edwina turned her attention once more to the stack of papers Bascomb had tasked her with organizing. A bill from the butcher in Portsmith. One for coal. Several recommendations on how best to remove a nest of rodents from the attic. One pointed observation on how to repair a leaking portion of the roof in the west wing.

That leak was undoubtedly dripping water at this moment. The storm outside showed no sign of abating and seemed worse than when Edwina had first arrived.

Organization must come first. She sorted the stack of papers into neat piles on the desk. A small portion were letters from Bascomb's acquaintances in London. One correspondence was from a farmer in Scotland who wanted to sell Bascomb some sheep. But there weren't any invitations for dinner or other social events. Given Rose Abbey's isolation, it was doubtful Bascomb had much of a social life. Anything having to do with maintaining the household—foodstuffs, supplies, and the like—Edwina put to the left. Correspondence of a more personal nature, she put in the middle. Related repairs to the abbey were put to the right and constituted the largest stack. Apparently, Rose Abbey had been left in poor condition until Bascomb had inherited it a little over a year ago. Nodding to herself, Edwina took in the neat piles, trying to decide where to begin. She dearly wished Fielding had left notes.

Perhaps he had.

Edwina opened the drawer of the desk and poked around. More string. Two buttons from a man's waistcoat, possibly Fielding's. A brass paperweight, which she immediately put to good use. Finally, her fingers closed over a small, leather-bound book.

Fielding *had* left notes. As had Worthington. Larkspur. And someone with the unfortunate name of Merrywimple. She leafed through the pages, noting the different handwriting and collections of dates. Notes had been made on finding stonemasons, roofers, and the like. And a priest.

A priest?

There was no indication from Merrywimple, who had made the notation, as to whether he'd found a priest or why he'd been looking for one.

Glancing out at the spikes of gravestones, barely visible in the rain and what little light remained of the day, Edwina could see some were very close to the edge of the cliff. Perhaps Merrywimple had been arranging for those graves to be moved and wanted a priest involved for religious reasons? She ran her finger down the remainder of his notes. Merrywimple had been the first of Bascomb's secretaries, lasting a total of two months before resigning.

Two months.

What would have made Merrywimple leave his position after such a short time? The isolation? Flipping through the pages, Edwina found Fielding's notes. His observations ran along mostly the same lines as the others Bascomb had employed. But Fielding had fled after only a few weeks. One notation jumped out at her.

Have portrait of Lady Renalda relocated to another part of Rose Abbey. I can't stand for her to look at me a moment longer.

Edwina glanced up from the desk to the abbess. Lady Renalda *was* mildly terrifying for a dead woman. And given the way she had perished and the rumors surrounding the abbey, Edwina could well understand why Fielding wouldn't want to share the library with her. Edwina doubted she was the only new arrival to Rose Abbey who had had to endure McDeaver's gruesome tales. But Lady Renalda's stern gaze still looked out over the library. Fielding hadn't won that argument with Bascomb.

The next entry was very curious indeed.

Ask Lord B about door in library.

Edwina's gaze settled on the two double doors leading into the room. There was nothing unusual. Carved wood. Brass knobs. The hinges didn't even squeak. Nothing appeared to be in need of repair. She frowned and turned back to the notes Fielding had made.

"Well, Collins. I see you aren't cowering in your room yet."

Edwina snapped shut Fielding's notes and shoved the small book back in the desk. "Not as of yet, my lord." She faced him. "But it is still early. There's time."

Bascomb gave her a stern look and walked into the library, immediately making the entire room smaller. His larger form dominated the space, filling the library with the scents of bergamot and something clean and undeniably masculine. Edwina hadn't been wrong. Bascomb was quite tall. Big. Like a massive, gnarled oak tree. The leather breeches he wore stretched taut across his thighs, showing Edwina the carved lines of muscle beneath. The long lengths of leg ended in immense, booted feet, which trod heavily in her direction.

Awareness trailed up Edwina's spine. Bascomb's effect on her hadn't dimmed in the least since their initial meeting. The chill was immediately banished from the library. If anything, Edwina felt overwarm.

Bascomb's gaze slid first to Edwina, then down at the tea tray. "Nicely done of Cook." One large paw reached out, snatching up two sandwiches. "Hearty."

Edwina watched the movement of his mouth as he ate, the bob of his throat as he swallowed. She had never found a man devouring a bit of roast beef to be quite so intriguing.

Dear God, what was wrong with her?

"Is something amiss, Collins?"

"Not in the least, my lord. I wanted to ask, What is the size of your staff at Rose Abbey? I didn't realize you had a cook—"

"How do you think I eat?" He frowned. "Mrs. Oates. Lovely woman. Did you think it was Page who did the cooking? She can't boil an egg."

"I'm curious why you have a housekeeper with only a cook, a maid—"

"And Thomas. Good lad. Lifts things. Like your trunk. Helps me with repairs and such. Mr. Oates, husband to my cook, takes care of the stables. They reside in a cottage a short walk from here." He raised a brow. "Is there a point to this discussion, Collins?"

"Not at all." Edwina kept her expression polite. "I was only trying to ascertain who was in your employ."

"Mrs. Page came with Rose Abbey, if you must know. She was my uncle's housekeeper. Perhaps something more," he said offhand. "I've never been clear on their relationship. Her mother served as housekeeper as well, to another Lord Bascomb. My uncle's grandfather, I believe. Very complicated family tree. At any rate, Mrs. Page deals with all the little details I don't care about, such as whether there's enough beeswax or clean linens. If you're looking at the household accounts, she is the person who knows best."

"Understandable." Mrs. Page had likely grown up at Rose Abbey if her mother had once been the housekeeper here.

"I see you've met Lady Renalda." Bascomb nodded at the portrait. "She was the last abbess to preside here. This was once her house, or at least part of it was. The library was her office."

"Mrs. Page told me as much. She said it was your family who made the renovations after being gifted the estate."

"'Gifted' is a bit of a stretch." His eyes were on Lady Renalda. "My ancestor performed a sordid service for the Crown. Rose Abbey was his reward. Did McDeaver leave that part out, Collins?"

Thunder boomed again.

A shiver dusted Edwina's skin. "The nuns were not treated kindly."

"No." Bascomb had a pained look on his face. "I find it shameful a relation of mine, no matter how far in the past, had a part in the murder of innocents. My ancestor had been promised a title and an estate"—he waved his arm around the room—"but first he had to evict an order of nuns and secure the wealth of Rose Abbey."

"What sort of wealth?" McDeaver had been vague on the details.

"Relics of a religious nature, I'd expect. Gold chalices. Silver crosses embedded with jewels. That sort of thing. There's no actual record of such wealth, but since Rose Abbey had never been raided as so many other monasteries and convents had, the assumption was made that there was a trove of gold plate and the like to be found here. However, when the soldiers and my ancestor arrived"—he gave her a sideways glance—"they found nothing but a determined abbess and her devoted flock."

"McDeaver claims Lady Renalda was overly prideful. That she refused to surrender to anyone but God. That their blood is on her hands. He made her sound very greedy."

Bascomb shrugged his massive shoulders, drawing Edwina's attention to the pull of the fine lawn along his arms. "My ancestor confronted Lady Renalda here, in this very room, while his soldiers scoured the grounds. Demanded she give over the abbey's wealth. She laughed in his face. He ordered the abbey and church set afire, hoping to force Lady Renalda to relent. Ordered his soldiers to kill anyone they came across."

Edwina imagined how frightening it all must have been. "Lady Renalda should have just surrendered."

"She didn't. Instead she kept my ancestor in this room with her, refusing to budge on her position, while everything behind her burned. Lady Renalda brandished a sword and was cut down," he said in a quiet voice. "But I don't think she was mad, Collins. Or prideful. Or any of the other things McDeaver probably made her out to be.

Her death, her sacrifice, was a diversion. She was buying time for the others." He looked up at Lady Renalda with something very much like admiration.

"The others?"

"Rose Abbey was once a small village on its own. Nearly thirty nuns and novices, along with a small group of orphans, resided here. Possibly more." He turned back to her. "I've looked at the archives. Only five nuns were executed with Lady Renalda. *Five.* No one else. Certainly no mention of orphaned children being slaughtered. I think it makes sense to assume that she gave orders for everyone else to escape while she kept that first Lord Bascomb and the soldiers occupied. I'm sure those innocents were long gone before the torch was put to the abbey."

"Where did they go?" Edwina's brow wrinkled. "There is only one way in and out of Rose Abbey. The road leading to Portsmith. Surely the soldiers would have blocked it."

Bascomb shrugged. "A mystery. The records show that the soldiers found no gold. No treasure. Not so much as a silver cross. The first Lord Bascomb searched for weeks and enlisted half the village to look. Eventually, he took possession of Rose Abbey and began adding to the home of the abbess."

"I find it a bit morbid that he wanted to keep the room she was murdered in and merely build around it."

Bascomb nodded. "Odd. Especially since he allowed the rest to go to rot. But I think the horror of what he'd done never left him. He even kept the portrait of Lady Renalda. Claimed to see her and the other nuns walking about the grounds. Rambled away like a madman."

Edwina looked up once more at the abbess. McDeaver had painted Lady Renalda in a very unflattering light, but Edwina supposed it was more fun to tell stories of a wrathful abbess than talk about this year's crop of wheat when a stranger visited Portsmith. A ghost story was much more amusing. "The villagers in Portsmith insist Rose Abbey is haunted."

"Oh, it is." Bascomb grabbed another sandwich and strolled to the doors. "Have a good evening, Collins."

Chapter Three

Edwina finished braiding the length of her hair, stretching out her neck and shoulders. She'd worked through the remainder of the afternoon and into the early evening, starting with the largest pile of Bascomb's papers. The receipts and correspondence pertaining to the restoration of the estate seemed the most urgent. Opening a ledger, she'd thought to start matching receipts with entries but stopped after seeing the mistakes sprinkled throughout the rows of numbers. Edwina was far too exhausted to begin what she could see at first glance would be quite a project.

The intensity of the storm outside hadn't abated a bit. Rain still lashed the windows with fury. She thought of Lady Renalda and the horrible events that had taken place at Rose Abbey so long ago. Bascomb's version of what had transpired here was likely closer to the truth than the tale spun by McDeaver. It pained Edwina to know that Lady Renalda, in addition to what she'd suffered in life, must also have the indignity of her good name besmirched in death.

Edwina sighed and looked out over the darkness cloaking the estate. She supposed it didn't matter what the truth was any longer. Everyone who had been involved was long dead. Despite Bascomb's parting words that Rose Abbey was haunted, Edwina didn't believe in ghosts.

The wind continued to howl and snake around the house, trying to find a space between the stones. Thankfully, Edwina's room seemed well insulated against the storm. The stone walls had to be a foot thick. The quarters Mrs. Page had directed her to were comfortable, if not large. The bed had a thick mattress, as fine as anything that had once graced her parents' home, complete with a canopy and bed-curtains. Fine fabrics, even if the style was out of date. A fire roared away in the hearth, spreading a comfortable glow across the room. Soap, towels, and a pitcher of warm water awaited her. She hadn't been hungry after the enormous tray of food served her earlier and had instead opted for a pot of chamomile tea when Meg had knocked softly at the door.

Lying back in the bed, Edwina left the curtains open a fraction to allow in the heat from the fire. Her fingers curled around the edges of the coverlet as she stared at the canopy above her head. Exhaustion settled in her bones, yet she was unable to fall asleep. Again, she considered the consequences of her somewhat rash decision to accept the position with Bascomb, though at the time, Edwina had thought it the best choice.

Since her father's death, Edwina had been stuck in a continuous cycle of survival. Her family's descent into poverty had been slow. Excruciating. Painful. Brought on by a combination of poor investments made by her father—which he'd tried to hide from her—and constant overspending by Edwina's frivolous mother. Father had refused to beg for charity from his relation, the Earl of Southwell, instead insisting that things would "turn around."

They never had.

Edwina had spent her days negotiating with the butcher. The dressmaker. The farmer from whom they'd purchased their eggs. She'd chopped wood for their fire. Decided the price of sugar was so dear that they would drink their tea without. Let go of their maid. Cook. The embarrassment of her family's decline was such that Edwina kept the worst of the situation from her cousin, the Earl of Southwell, as well as other members of their far-flung family. Edwina was mortified. Especially after her broken betrothal. When she'd finally been forced to sell the family home, Edwina had taken what coins she'd had left and arrived at Southwell's estate, the advertisement from Bascomb clutched in one hand. Edwina had begged Southwell to write her a recommendation, explaining she wanted to make her own way in the world. She was too ashamed to confess the true state of her affairs.

Southwell, she'd pleaded, need only help her with this small thing.

Southwell had written the recommendation, against his better judgment. He'd told Edwina she could work for him, if she were so determined to be a secretary, but Edwina had refused.

Now, listening to the wind howl outside, Edwina thought perhaps she would have been better off cataloging Southwell's collection of stone tablets, pottery, and terrifying masks.

He had quite a lot of those.

But Edwina hadn't wanted charity. Marriage certainly was no longer an option. Suitors did not bang on the door of Miss Edwina Collins, poor spinster. She wasn't even a maid anymore thanks to her mildly satisfying affair with the barrister whose offer of marriage she'd accepted. Of course, that was before the Honorable Jacob Duster had realized he would be getting nothing but Edwina and had withdrawn his offer.

Hands clenched, she thumped the mattress.

His abandonment still smarted. She'd been wildly attracted to Duster. Experienced a decent amount of pleasure in his arms, which had boded well for their marriage. Edwina thought Duster cared for her. That there was true affection between them. Yet when he'd realized the circumstances of the Collins family, Duster had broken off their relationship by sending a note to Edwina's father.

Hadn't even had the decency to inform Edwina himself.

"So now I'm here. Trapped at Rose Abbey with a—man I shouldn't find the least attractive. And one with whom I should retain a professional relationship and nothing more." Bascomb made every nerve in Edwina's body stand at attention with those unusual eyes and striking looks. The attraction between them had crackled in the air when Bascomb had visited her earlier in the library. Her pulse skipped at the thought of him touching her.

Damn it.

Frowning, she plumped her pillow, pulled the blankets up to her chin, and firmly shut her eyes. She was here to be Bascomb's secretary. Nothing more.

Chapter Four

Edwina woke slowly, keeping her eyes closed. Wind still threw rain against the windows. The sound of waves crashing against the cliffs was a distant roar. The fire, now little more than banked embers, popped and hissed.

Something was dragging along the floor of her room. Like a wet mop just out of the bucket. Or thick, soaked skirts slapping against flesh.

She was not alone.

The air in Edwina's chest froze. Her lungs refused to work properly. Blind terror, the sort made of nightmares and darkness, shot through her body. Edwina couldn't move even if she wanted to. It was all she could do to resist the scream clawing up her throat.

Keep breathing, Edwina. Pretend to be asleep.

The bed-curtains fluttered, the sound reaching her terrified ears. Ice-cold air brushed over the curve of her shoulder and teased at her hair. She struggled to keep her breathing even as the sensation of someone leaning over her pressed against her skin.

I am going to scream my bloody head off.

Just as quickly, the heaviness eased, followed by the sensation of fingers stroking the back of her head, as Edwina's mother used to do. The choking fear abated, supplanted by a sense of peace and comfort. She drew in a soft breath and opened her eyes, unsurprised to find herself completely alone, the bed-curtains undisturbed.

Edwina sat up, pulling aside the edge of the velvet curtain to survey the room. Nothing whatsoever stirred. There wasn't even a draft from the windows. The air in the room was cool but not the icy blast she'd felt along her shoulder.

Forcing herself out of the bed, Edwina checked to see that her door was still locked. She made the daring move of looking beneath the bed as she had when she was a child. To search for monsters.

Nothing.

Edwina drew in a shaky breath. "I was dreaming. A nightmare. Nothing more," she said out loud to the stillness of the room. Again, she cursed McDeaver and his macabre stories. Turning back to the warmth of the bed, Edwina halted. Roses. The scent permeated the entire room, as if someone had filled a dozen vases with nothing but the bloodred blooms that sprawled all over the grounds of Rose Abbey.

"I don't believe in ghosts," she chanted to herself. "A bad dream, nothing more." Edwina looked around the room. One small crimson rose petal lay on the table next to her empty teacup.

Edwina clasped her trembling hands together. Meg must have been arranging flowers. A petal dropped on the tray before she brought the tea to Edwina. She only hadn't noticed the petal earlier.

Cautiously, still scanning her room, Edwina crawled back into bed, pulling the covers up to her chin. She thought of the portrait of the abbess. And the spray of bloodred roses lying in her lap.

It was a very long time before Edwina fell asleep once more.

Chapter Five

"Ah, there you are, Collins," Lord Bascomb, with a piece of ham dangling from his raised fork, greeted her as she entered the breakfast room the following morning. "Wondered when you would make an appearance."

"Good morning, my lord," Edwina answered, taking a seat.

Meg had knocked on her door earlier, informing Edwina that Lord Bascomb had requested her presence in the breakfast room. She was somewhat surprised to find that her employer expected them to eat together, but Bascomb didn't seem the sort to stand on ceremony. There was no reason to at Rose Abbey, she supposed. Or possibly he didn't wish to eat alone.

Atop the sideboard sat an enormous amount of food that Bascomb, if the two empty plates before him were any indication, was intent on devouring all on his own. The thick mass of inky hair brushed against the breadth of his shoulders as he ate, the ends curling into his collar. No cravat or coat once more. And he was in dire need of a closer shave.

There had been no mention of a valet earlier when he'd listed the staff of Rose Abbey, and from Bascomb's rough appearance, it was clear he didn't have one.

How odd. He is a titled lord. A gentleman.

Edwina narrowed her eyes. Titled he may be, but Bascomb was no gentleman, not with his apparent dislike of cravats and manners.

A tiny shiver trailed down her spine. It was not unpleasant.

"I expected you down earlier, Collins." His eyes, more gray than green in the morning light, peered back at her. "Did the storm keep you awake? Or perhaps—" He hesitated. "—it was something else?"

If Bascomb thought she would admit to an imaginary hand stroking her hair and filling her room with the scent of roses, he was sorely mistaken. "Exhaustion, my lord. I do apologize. The journey to Rose Abbey was lengthy. I merely overslept."

"That was Fielding's room. And Worthington's." He tapped his finger. "Come to think of it, I believe Mrs. Page has put each of my secretaries there. Easier, I suppose, to keep one room at the ready." He leaned forward slightly, the collar of his shirt gaping open to show a delectable slice of male skin. "You do look refreshed, Collins."

It was difficult to concentrate when Bascomb was so distracting. Or at least, *parts* of him were distracting. She caught the smells of bergamot and soap in the air around him, which made her skin tingle once more. "I am, my lord."

Edwina placed a piece of toast on her plate.

"You'll faint well before tea if that's all you're going to eat." Bascomb stole a glance out the window, sighing in resignation. "And I suppose you *will* be here for tea. Can't send you back to Hampshire today as I wished, Collins." A tiny smirk lifted his lips. "The storm hasn't stopped. But as soon as the rain abates and the roads are clear, off you go."

"Of course, my lord." Edwina sipped her tea, savoring the burn against her tongue. "I would expect as much."

Bascomb tore into another piece of ham. "Is that sarcasm, Collins?"

"Not at all, my lord, merely agreement." She nibbled at her toast.

His gazed lowered, focusing solely on her mouth.

Edwina had trouble swallowing and told herself it was the dry texture of her breakfast. She dribbled some honey over the top of the toast. As she took another bite, a bit of honey slid across her lips, and she caught the drop with her tongue.

Bascomb made a feral noise. His eyes full of heat and the promise of wicked things raised to hers.

The attraction between them, so immediate and unexpected, threatened to combust, right here in the small breakfast room. A vision of Bascomb, pressing Edwina down atop the breakfast table and lifting her skirts, was so vivid she nearly dropped her toast.

Mrs. Page bustled in without knocking, and Edwina hastily dropped her eyes to her plate, pulse racing. For the first time since coming to Rose Abbey, Edwina actually welcomed the woman's presence.

"My lord," the housekeeper announced, "the leak in the east wing has grown exponentially larger according to Thomas. I believe several tiles have flown off the roof, threatening the guest room at the end of the third floor. Your attention is required." A tiny nod of her chin was the only acknowledgment of Edwina's presence.

"Very well, Mrs. Page, though I've yet to finish breakfast."

Mrs. Page glanced at Bascomb's empty plates with a dubious look.

"Tell Thomas to grab the necessary tools, and I'll be along in a moment." He dismissed her with a wave. "I won't have time at present, Collins, to review your work. I will have to trust it is acceptable."

"I've sorted through a great deal of your correspondence and will start on the ledgers today," Edwina replied.

"So soon?" Bascomb's face held a look of surprise. "It took Fielding nearly a week to sort through everything."

"Perhaps Fielding wasn't proficient at balancing estate ledgers or household accounts. I am." Edwina patted her lips with a napkin.

Mrs. Page smoothed her skirts, eyeing Edwina with one brow raised in disbelief.

Well, Edwina didn't give a fig for the housekeeper's opinion.

"Is there anything else, Mrs. Page?" Bascomb muttered. "Or do you wish to stand there and watch me eat the remainder of my breakfast?"

Mrs. Page's face tightened at the rebuke from her employer. "I only wished to inform Miss Collins that I've already had the fire lit in the library should she wish to begin her work directly after breakfast. I'll have a tea brought later."

Bascomb rolled his eyes. "Don't coddle Collins." His eyes swept over Edwina. "She doesn't require it. And make sure the contents of the tea tray are *hearty*, Mrs. Page. None of those silly little iced biscuits Mrs. Oates likes to make. Collins will waste away eating nothing but bits of toast. It's barely enough to keep a mouse alive."

"Of course, my lord." Mrs. Page bobbed politely and finally left the room, closing the door behind her.

"I'm not overly fond of breakfast, my lord," Edwina said, finding it necessary to explain why she wasn't tucking into the ham and eggs as Bascomb did.

"Neither am I." He sopped up a bit of egg with his toast.

"Yes," she replied smoothly. "It becomes more apparent by the moment."

Bascomb grunted in annoyance, though amusement lit his gray-green eyes. "You're not endearing yourself to me, Collins. Certainly you haven't made friends with Mrs. Page. Not entirely your fault, Collins. She hasn't liked any of my secretaries. Detested Merryfort."

"Merrywimple." Edwina corrected.

"My mistake." Bascomb was stunning when he smiled, as he was doing now. A soft, buttery glow spread across her midsection. The awareness of him returned, fiercer than before the appearance of Mrs. Page.

"Didn't like Fielding either. Tolerated Worthless."

"Worthington, my lord." Edwina bit her lip to keep from grinning. Bascomb was trying to make her lose her composure. "You're botching their names on purpose, I think. I'm curious, my lord. Why didn't Mrs. Page like your previous secretaries?"

"Mrs. Page doesn't like anyone, including me, Collins. Surely you've noticed. Tolerating is not liking. One of the stipulations of the inheritance of Rose Abbey was her continued employment as housekeeper indefinitely. I can't dismiss her. My uncle made sure of it. As previously mentioned"—his voiced lowered as if they were conspirators—"I believe Mrs. Page and my uncle were…quite close. If you take my meaning."

Bascomb was terrible to suggest such a thing. But likely correct. It explained a great deal about the housekeeper's proprietary attitude about the estate. "I do, my lord."

"As to the ledgers, Fielding was terrible. Complained nonstop about missing bills of sale, incorrect notations, and the like. Constantly bothered Mrs. Page for receipts. Pestered her with questions on what purchases had been made for the household. I'm sure she was relieved when Fielding fled down the hill, never to return."

Edwina thought carefully about her next words. "Did you review the accounts yourself, my lord, and find irregularities?"

Bascomb rubbed at the spot where the scar sprouted from his left eye with one large finger. "When I have time." His tone was defensive. "Which is rare."

She nodded in polite understanding. Bascomb wasn't looking at his own accounts; that much was clear.

"I rarely have time, Collins," he snapped at her. "Which is why I need a secretary. A competent one. But I suppose you'll do for the moment."

Edwina didn't flinch from his anger, knowing that it wasn't truly directed at her but himself. The scar told her Bascomb had suffered a head injury of some sort, possibly one bad enough that it affected his ability to read the ledgers or, at the very least, be able to discern any inaccuracies. "Your scar, my lord. May I ask how you came to have it?"

His lips twisted, the man no doubt about to snap at her once more, but a great sigh escaped his lips instead. Blunt fingers tossed down the napkin. "You may. It is no great secret. Scything incident."

"Scything?" Edwina had suspected a duel with swords possibly or a fall from his horse.

"Yes. Scything." One long arm made a sweeping motion across the table. "Come now, Collins, surely you understand the point. The cutting of wheat. A tradition for the sons of my family to cut the first shaft of wheat for the harvest. My older brother managed to do so without injuring himself. And my younger. I, however, was not so lucky." The broad shoulders shrugged. "A rat the size of a bloody goat ran over my foot. I must have jumped nearly a foot into the air, stumbled over a rock—which should not have been in the field to begin with—and fell. So did the blade. Nearly lost the eye. Cheek flayed open. Blood everywhere. My mother screaming her head off." Bascomb shook his head. "Not my finest day."

"A rat the size of a goat? My goodness, I hadn't realized a rodent could grow to such a size. You're fortunate you weren't trampled as well if that is the case."

"No sympathy, Collins? I expected a tiny bit."

Edwina sincerely doubted that. Bascomb didn't strike her as the sort of man who would welcome pity because of his injury.

"You have a quick wit, Collins. Fielding did not. Nor Worthless."

"Worthington," she corrected, wondering why she bothered. "A point in my favor, I suppose."

"You also didn't run screaming out of the house last night," Bascomb said with grudging approval. "Another mark of your brief success at Rose Abbey thus far."

"It was raining." A small pebble of unease formed as she thought of the dream she'd had last night. The sensation of having her hair stroked, as if Edwina was a child in need of comfort. The scent of roses in the air. She hadn't imagined any of it. Or had a nightmare. Truthfully, Rose Abbey unnerved Edwina as it doubtless had every other secretary. Fielding, for instance. The house and its inhabitants weren't exactly warm and welcoming.

"When you're done with the ledgers, Collins, the library should be next."

"The library?" Edwina wanted to ask more about Bascomb's injury and the lack of attention to the ledgers but decided he'd changed the topic on purpose. "What is there to be done to the library?"

"Cataloging, Collins. The attic is filled with crates, all containing books. I have no idea which relation of mine sent them to Rose Abbey or why. Most of them have probably turned to dust, which should save you some time." Bascomb stood, looming over Edwina, large and male. Smelling of bergamot and soap. Her gaze traveled over the line of his throat and the hard line of his jaw.

"I do hope"—Edwina quickly looked away, instructing her pulse to settle—"that I'll be able to complete both tasks before you send me back to Hampshire tomorrow, my lord."

His tall form bent, leaning so close Edwina could have sworn she felt the brush of lips against the curve of her ear. A delicious, decadent sensation coursed down her spine, all thoughts of the ledgers and her nightmare forgotten. How could she have formed such a strong attachment to him so quickly? Every nerve in her body was standing on end.

"Then you should get started, Collins." The husky words scraped against her skin, and it was far too early to be aroused while eating toast. "As quickly as possible."

Chapter Six

Edwina lifted her head from the ledgers she'd spent the better part of the day poring over, stretching her neck until the bones made a satisfying pop. The rain continued to beat against the walls of Rose Abbey in a continuous rhythm. Even if the weather let up this instant, the roads would remain muddy and unsuitable for travel for several days. Enough time, Edwina hoped, to convince Bascomb to keep her on. She certainly couldn't do any worse a job than any of the previous secretaries he'd hired. The ledgers were a mess. Small mistakes abounded. So many secretaries had touched the ledgers that almost none of the handwriting matched, making it difficult to discern where the errors originated. Or who had made them.

Edwina found the last bit far more interesting.

Extensive repairs were being done at Rose Abbey, a process that had started with the current Lord Bascomb's uncle. Oddly enough, it wasn't the older part of the house that required the attention, but the wing onto which each successive Lord Bascomb had added.

Ironic. Lady Renalda's residence still stood, while her conqueror's was in a constant state of repair.

Edwina resettled herself at the desk, nibbling on a bit of apple and cheese Meg had brought a short time ago. There had been at least three different stonemasons who'd made repairs to Rose Abbey. Opening the ledger, she paged back to Merrywimple's notes, which had first made mention of the work.

The thud of a book echoed in the silence of the library.

Edwina's head jerked up, her gaze immediately settling on a darkened corner by the window, the same spot where she'd found the fallen books yesterday. The noise was likely the result of an uneven shelf. The thunder outside had started up again, shaking the house. It was no stretch to assume the vibrations would knock a book off the shelf.

Ignoring the interruption, Edwina bent her head once more to the task at hand. She picked up the bill from the first stonemason, a man named Jeffers, and looked back at the ledger.

The amount noted was larger than the payment requested by Jeffers. Not by a great deal. Barely noticeable. Obviously an oversight.

Another book dropped.

Edwina didn't look up. She would mention to Bascomb the need to reinforce the shelves on that particular bookcase.

A leather tome flew across the room, hitting the pot of tea on the desk, knocking everything to the floor.

Edwina jolted from her seat as tea stained the rug. She picked up the knife she'd been using to peel the apple. A poor weapon only marginally better than the pen. Ghosts, as far as she knew, did not throw books with incredible accuracy.

The house was deadly silent around her. Then she heard it. A heavy whisper as if someone or something moved between the bookcases.

She wasn't alone in the library.

"I don't find this the least amusing. Show yourself." Heart racing, Edwina marched over to the corner, knife raised, and stepped around the bookshelf. Lightning zigzagged outside, bathing the ruins of the abbey and this dark corner of the library in a streak of white light.

The room was empty. Silent. Except for the sound of her own ragged breathing.

Get ahold of yourself Edwina.

A loud creak echoed in the silence. She turned in time to see an entire wall of books tumbling toward her. A hand shoved hard against Edwina's back. The bookcase crashed to the floor, only managing to catch the very edge of her shoulder instead of landing on top of her. Wincing at the sharp pain in her shoulder, she had the presence of mind to squeeze herself flush against the windows as the bookcase fell to the floor, dust rising into the air.

Edwina pressed herself as tightly as she could against the window, the knife clasped to her chest, startled with the shock of nearly being crushed under the weight of hundreds of books. Hand trembling, weapon held aloft, she darted her gaze about, searching for any movement in the library.

The tang of roses filled the air, pushing away the smells of mold and dust.

Her gaze jerked to the portrait of Lady Renalda, calmly watching from above the fireplace. Pushing away from the window, Edwina carefully made her way to the desk, dropping the knife with a small clatter. The overturned teapot on the floor lay on its side, the tea having made a large stain on the rug.

"A fresh pot of tea is definitely in order," she said out loud. "Or brandy."

Straightening, Edwina commanded her feet to move in the direction of the door. Bascomb must have brandy in his study. Or something equally bracing. Surely he wouldn't begrudge her, not after having nearly been killed.

Her hand went to her midsection.

Once the shock wore off, she would find Mrs. Page and inform the housekeeper there had been an accident in the library.

Chapter Seven

"What do you mean, Collins, the bookcase just fell over?" Bascomb shot her a look. "It's bolted into the wall."

Edwina sat in the overstuffed settee and sipped at her brandy-laced tea. She'd poured part of the bottle straight into the teapot, and now that Bascomb was in the library, she hoped he wouldn't ask for a cup. The brandy had thankfully calmed her nerves. Somewhat. At least she wasn't trembling anymore. Looking down at the damask-upholstered settee, Edwina decided she really detested the pattern.

"Collins." Bascomb snapped his fingers at her.

"Bolted or not, the bookcase fell. Nearly on top of me. Perhaps the floor is uneven or the age of the wood caused one of the shelves to simply come apart. The wood does look rather ancient." It was none of those things as Edwina well knew. The bookcase had fallen with the intent to crush her. If she hadn't moved to the side at the last minute—

But I didn't. I was pushed *out of the way.* And the smell of roses had been everywhere, mixing with those of dust and leather.

Edwina looked up from her tea to regard the portrait of Lady Renalda and the roses the abbess held in her lap. "Who planted all the rosebushes at Rose Abbey?"

"What?" Bascomb was examining the wall and the bookcase.

"The roses. Who planted them?"

"The nuns, I suppose." He frowned. "The bolts must have come loose. The wood of the bookcase isn't splintered. Strange, it looks like there should be four bolts attaching the bookcase, but two are missing and the others just pulled free."

Edwina raised her head. "Bolts?"

"The end was bolted to the wall here." His hand trailed down the stone. "Possibly the vibration from the thunder loosened them, but—" He shook his head and came over to Edwina, the cushions of the settee dipping as his larger form settled next to her. Bascomb was far too close than was proper or necessary, a muscled thigh nearly touching her skirts.

Edwina had the inclination to lean into him, which would not do.

"Are you hurt, Collins?" There was genuine concern written in Bascomb's sharply hewn features, softening the edges of the scar and making him far more attractive than Edwina wished him to be. One big hand stretched out across the hideous damask of the settee, the tip of his forefinger running along the edge of her skirts.

"No, my lord." Edwina, heat flooding her cheeks, had to look away from the sight of that big, blunt finger. She wanted him to touch her.

Oh, Edwina. You've had too much brandy.

"I was only a bit shaken," she assured him, deciding not to mention the pain in her shoulder or the fact that something had pushed her out of the way.

"I'm sure availing yourself of my best brandy has helped."

"It was for medicinal purposes." She paused, wondering if she should mention the book that had flown across the room and knocked over the teapot, but she decided against it. Bascomb might think her addled, or worse, assume she was foxed.

I very nearly am.

She took another sip of her tea, allowing the taste to settle on her tongue before continuing. "I heard a thud near the bookcase and went to investigate. There was a crack of thunder along with a great deal of lightning. The wood creaked as it fell over. I—I thought I heard someone walking around." A small chuckle escaped her. "Perhaps a joke was being played on me."

"A very poor one." Bascomb's eyes fairly glowed in the dim light of the library. They really were quite extraordinary. Looking at them was like losing oneself in the depths of a forest during a storm.

"You look a bit dazed, Collins. Are you sure you didn't hit your head?"

"It's only that you possess the loveliest eyes. Such an unusual color." Edwina winced. She sounded like a young girl mooning over her first beau. The brandy was to blame.

Bascomb shook his head and took the tea out of her hands, sniffed at the dark brew, and set it aside. "No more of that. I've no desire to carry you upstairs to bed."

Edwina's entire body pulsed in response.

He stilled, possibly realizing the undercurrent in his words, but he didn't try to apologize or rephrase his statement. Instead, his eyes darkened to a deep, mossy green.

She clasped her hands in her lap, looking down at her fingers, trying to stop the arousal from sliding up her legs. Impossible with Bascomb so close and the brandy muddling her brain.

"Fielding hated the library." His words helped banish the tension between them. "He wanted me to take down her portrait." Bascomb nodded to Lady Renalda. "I refused. Didn't seem right. This was her office, after all, before one of my ancestors made the room a library."

"Mrs. Page informed me. You admire the abbess," Edwina said quietly. "You don't think she's a vengeful spirit."

"Fielding"—Bascomb ignored her observation—"heard things as well. A book flew through the air and hit him in the head. He said there were footsteps shuffling behind him while he worked. I told him it was only mice crawling about in the spaces in the walls."

The walls of this part of Rose Abbey were stone. Edwina decided not to mention the fact. Otherwise, the description of what Fielding had endured matched almost exactly Edwina's earlier experience.

"He claimed to see the figure of a woman wandering outside, fluttering in the ruins of the abbey."

"Fluttering?"

"Floating." Bascomb waved his hand. "Hovering. A ghastly pale figure. Hands stretched toward this room, beseeching Fielding. Said the ghost visited him in his room. Rattled the door. Scraped her nails against the wood. When he opened the doors, the specter floated down the hall away from him."

Her brow wrinkled. Whatever had been in her room last night had been momentarily terrifying but hadn't attempted to harm her. Instead, she'd been comforted. No scraping of nails, just the odd, damp sound moving across the floor.

"I've seen nothing at all like that, my lord." Technically it wasn't a lie.

"Larkspur claimed a ghostly nun roamed about the remains of the abbey at night. Lights bobbed around the graveyard and church. Merrywimple heard things too. Insisted he saw orbs around the church. Called them spirit lights. Probably just treasure hunters looking for the wealth everyone assumes is in the church. I should have the stones all taken down and the graveyard fenced off. The story of Rose Abbey's wealth is well known in Portsmith along with the rest of the tale. But only Worthless—"

"Worthington," Edwina corrected him.

"—and Fielding claimed to be attacked by the ghost." He looked once more at the books strewn across the library. *"Worthington,"* he emphasized, "insisted the ghost of Lady Renalda tried to push him down the stairs after he followed the specter out of his room." His massive shoulders gave a roll. "He was a highly excitable, odd young man."

The briefest whiff of bergamot met her nostrils, stirring Edwina's insides in a pleasant manner. It must be the soap he used to wash, for it certainly couldn't be shaving soap. Bascomb didn't seem to shave as often as he should.

"I saw nothing here before the bookcase fell. There was an odd shuffling sound in the corner. But I doubt any ghost, even one as fierce as Lady Renalda, has the strength to push over such a heavy bookcase whether the bolts are loose or not." Edwina thought again about the book flying through the air toward the teapot. If it was Lady Renalda, she had excellent aim.

"I'm glad to hear it."

She didn't know why she was so reticent to tell Bascomb everything, but Edwina thought it best, for the time being, to keep the exact details to herself. Not because she didn't want to tell her employer, but because Edwina wasn't sure who else might be listening. "I should get back to the ledgers, my lord." She wobbled slightly as she came to her feet.

Bascomb caught her arm. "Are you certain you can make out the numbers after enjoying so much…tea?"

"Positive. I'm perfectly well." Bascomb's touch sent a jolt of heat up her arm.

"I am relieved," he hummed softly, blunt fingers curled tighter around her elbow, "that you are unhurt, Collins." His full lips tilted at one side in the semblance of a smile. "After all, I would hate for you to be injured when I send you back to Hampshire. The ride down the hill in McDeaver's pony cart would be uncomfortable if you were bruised."

Edwina bit back her own smile. "Very sound reasoning, my lord. I must get back to work promptly if I am to finish."

"I also have a decent bottle of whiskey in my study should you tire of brandy"—the words, low and deep, sent a vibration across her skin—"or require comfort at a later time." Bascomb's gaze dropped to her mouth. His jaw tilted in her direction.

The lovely, buttery sensation from earlier spilled once again down the length of Edwina's body, causing her to arch, just slightly, in his direction. Did Bascomb mean to kiss her? It certainly seemed—

Instead, he slowly released her arm, eyes still on her mouth as if he was fascinated by her lips, but there was also wariness. "Carry on, Collins," he said in a harsh tone before stepping away, putting a more appropriate distance between them. "And stay away from the bookcases until I can have this all cleaned up."

"Of course, my lord," she replied, watching as he shut the door behind him.

Edwina sat back down at the desk, heart beating wildly. It was unwise to become involved with one's employer. The idea was far more terrifying than being nearly crushed by a bookcase. Edwina doubted any encounter with Bascomb would end with only a kiss.

She took up the ledger once more and reached for the stack of receipts from Jeffers she'd been studying when the bookcase fell. The space was bare.

Looking down, she checked the floor, but there was nothing except a slight wet spot from where Meg had mopped up the tea.

The receipts were gone.

Chapter Eight

On Edwina's fourth day at Rose Abbey, the rain finally slowed to a misty drizzle. The sky remained overcast, with only a bare hint of gray light seeping through the clouds. Edwina had slept well the previous night, as she had every night since the incident in the library. Nothing disturbed her. Well, if one didn't count the highly erotic dreams Edwina was having about Bascomb. Naked, wicked images of them together, his big hands roaming over her body. She'd awoken this morning flushed and aroused, the space between her thighs aching.

Making her way to the breakfast room, Edwina was unsurprised to find Bascomb enjoying his usual large breakfast. What did surprise her was that he was in the breakfast room at all. He'd not been present yesterday, and Edwina had eaten alone. She'd thought it likely his avoidance of her had something to do with the kiss they'd very nearly shared. Wise of him.

An enormous plate of scrambled eggs sat before Bascomb, two thick slices of ham hanging off the edge of his plate. His gray-green eyes trailed over Edwina in annoyance.

"The rain has nearly stopped," he grumbled, pointing the fork at the window. "Hope you haven't unpacked, Collins."

Not much of a greeting. She would have preferred a cheery good morning. "Of course not, my lord." Edwina sipped her tea. "Perish the thought. I'm ready to leave at a moment's notice."

Her employer made a noncommittal grunt, scowling at her from across the table.

Edwina lifted her chin. "Is there something else, my lord?"

He cleared his throat and looked down at his eggs. Small touches of pink shone on the curves of his cheeks. "Are you well this morning? I was busy yesterday and didn't—"

"Very well, my lord," she interrupted.

Bascomb raised his eyes back to her. The green was more pronounced today. The color of leaves at the first sign of spring. "I've been busy making repairs in the east wing. Water leaks have sprouted in nearly every room. I've not had time to check on your progress."

"Everything is well in hand," she assured him.

They stared at each other for a moment, long enough for warmth to crawl between Edwina's breasts and settle low in her belly.

"Thomas will put the library back to rights once he's finished helping me, Collins." Bascomb stood, rather abruptly, and laid down his napkin. Longing flashed briefly in the depths of green, and Edwina did not think it was for more eggs. "You should get to work. Be…careful, Collins."

"Yes, my lord."

Edwina sipped her tea and picked absently at a piece of toast as the sound of his footsteps faded. Once the room grew silent again, she made her way to the library, balancing the cup of tea in her hand. She wasn't at all sure how to handle the attraction between them, and apparently, neither did Bascomb. Yes, she was physically drawn to him, but Edwina also found she liked Bascomb. Quite a bit.

Settling in at her desk, Edwina shuffled the papers, searching through the desk drawers again for the receipts from Jeffers. The other day, after the bookcase had fallen and she'd comforted herself with brandy, Edwina had thought she'd only misplaced the small pile. Tucked it in a drawer when the bookcase fell and didn't recall doing so. She'd been so shaken by the incident anything was possible. The last day or so, she'd focused on answering correspondence and organizing the remainder of Bascomb's receipts. But this morning, as the toes of her half boots hit the bottom of the desk, it occurred to Edwina she hadn't looked *there*.

Getting on her hands and knees, Edwina looked at the space between the floor and the bottom of the desk. Large enough for papers to flutter under. Reaching beneath the desk, she wiggled her fingers about for a slip of paper.

Mrs. Page certainly wasn't doing her due diligence in the library. The floor under the desk was thick with dust.

As she withdrew her hand in frustration, Edwina's fingers stuck on something damp. She pulled back her hand with a frown. A *leaf*. More correctly, the leaf of a rosebush. Still wet, with a bit of mud on the edge. Edwina sat back on the rug, staring at the leaf.

How did this get in here? She looked up at the large windows, all firmly latched. She wasn't even sure they *could* open. Had one of the panes broken during the storm?

Ask Lord B about door in library.

Fielding's odd notation echoed in her mind. Door. Not *doors*. The library entrance consisted of *two* solid double doors. Was there another entrance to the library?

"Miss Collins?"

Edwina gasped at the voice so close to her ear, turning her neck to see a pair of pleasant, if slightly vacant, brown eyes. A young man, built like a bull, stood before her. A thatch of blond hair, ends sticking out over his ears, covered his head.

"Thomas, I assume?"

The giant nodded. "Yes, Miss Collins."

"Goodness, you startled me." She came to her feet, a bit awkwardly, and brushed off her skirts. "There's quite a bit of dust beneath the desk." A sneeze threatened, and she pushed a finger to her nose. "I lost a button," she lied.

"Sorry, Miss Collins." Thomas spoke slowly, as if considering each word with care. He was square-jawed, with a thick neck and massive shoulders. "I'm done with the roof," he said by way of explaining his appearance. "Lord Bascomb told me to pick up the bookcase and books." A tentative smile crossed his lips. "And I'm not to disturb you."

"You won't, Thomas. I would appreciate your assistance." She tucked the leaf in the palm of her hand. "Thank you."

Thomas lumbered over to the bookcase, steps echoing in the quiet of the library. He kept his eyes averted from the portrait of the abbess.

"I'm not sure what happened, exactly," she said, watching as he lifted the heavy wood with ease, as if it weighed nothing. "Lord Bascomb thinks the bolts may have loosened over time."

"Rose Abbey is very…old. Things break. Holes in the roof. I fix everything with my tools."

There was something childlike about Thomas, as if his body had far outgrown his mind. "I'm sorry we weren't properly introduced when I arrived, Thomas. Lord Bascomb must keep you quite busy."

"Yes, Miss Collins." Thomas proceeded to move the bookcase back toward its original position. "I like to be busy." He began stacking the books neatly on the floor, running his hands over the rug, possibly searching for the mysterious bolts that had come loose.

Edwina knelt next to him, helping pick up the books. "Let me help. It's the least I can do. I'm sure the bolts merely rusted after so long. The vibration from the storm helped—"

"You should leave," Thomas interrupted her, one broad hand stretched over the stack of books in front of him. "It isn't safe for you." Soft brown eyes flitted to hers, the pleasant, vacant smile gone to be replaced by trembling lips. "She doesn't like new people," Thomas whispered. "Especially not the secretaries."

"Who? Mrs. Page?" Edwina hadn't thought Mrs. Page's dislike of her to be so glaring.

"No." Thomas shook his head. "The abbess."

Edwina looked him directly in the eye. "I don't believe in ghosts, Thomas. And you shouldn't either."

"You will," he said under his breath.

Edwina stood and went back to the desk, unsettled by Thomas and his words. He seemed a simple, kind man. Concerned for her. But she was not about to tolerate any more nonsense about the abbess haunting Rose Abbey, despite what she'd experienced.

Thomas said nothing else as he picked up the remainder of the books. He bowed before Edwina, informing her he'd be back later with tools to reattach the bookcase.

She went back to work, focusing on the ledgers, going through each column carefully. After a few hours, Edwina stretched her arms back, wondering at the inconsistencies. Reaching into the depths of the desk, she retrieved the small book containing the notes of her predecessors. The book fell open to Fielding's entry about the door.

She'd meant to ask Bascomb but forgotten. The note probably meant nothing, but Edwina didn't quite believe that. She glanced around the room and took the wet leaf out of her pocket where she'd stashed it when Thomas arrived. The leaf shouldn't have been in the library at all, let alone beneath the desk. According to Bascomb, he thought Lady Renalda had faced off with the soldiers in her office deliberately, to give the other residents of Rose Abbey time to flee. She must have known the soldiers would kill every last one of those under her care in their search for what gold they assumed the abbey possessed.

Edwina walked to the longest wall, running her hand along the bookcase. Ancient castles and old homes such as this were riddled with passages, priest holes, and hidden rooms. It wasn't far-fetched to think there would have been a secret passage from this room that led to the abbey or the church outside.

Or possibly the beach below the cliffs.

Edwina looked at the ruins sprawled out toward the edge of the cliff. She would bet her best petticoat that the way out of Rose Abbey led to the beach or possibly into the woods. The original builders of the abbey would have considered how best to hide themselves or escape if faced with a fleet of Viking longships.

Fielding must have found a hidden door. Pity he hadn't bothered to mention *where* in his notes.

"I would have imagined after your last encounter with a wall of books you'd avoid them entirely."

Edwina turned to see Bascomb, leaning against the doorjamb, watching her. His earlier annoyance seemed to have faded; in fact, Edwina would have said he appeared pleased to see her.

His gray-green eyes drifted over her bosom for a moment before coming back to her face.

"Checking on me, my lord?"

"Perhaps. Or possibly I'm merely hungry." He nodded to the tray Meg had brought earlier. Pushing up from the door, Bascomb passed Edwina to look out the window. Pacing before the glass, he absently pushed back a wave of inky hair from his brow, all the while giving Edwina an excellent view of his backside and the long, muscular lines of his legs. It was akin to watching a large bear prowl about.

Longing trailed over her skin. Desire the likes of which she'd never known. It was becoming incredibly problematic.

"How are the ledgers coming along?"

"Quite well, my lord." More inconsistencies had been discovered. All varied and spread out over the ledgers of each secretary's brief period of employment, done in such a way that one automatically would assume the person before one had merely made a mistake. Each secretary's handwriting was different, making it impossible to tell who had made specific entries and when. And with no one person checking the ledgers, as Bascomb should, it presented the perfect opportunity.

Perhaps Edwina had far more experience in ledgers being doctored, for she'd seen her father make the same sort of "mistakes" to hide the family's financial situation. Earlier, in reviewing the ledgers, she'd seen notations from yet another stonemason named Hodges. The ledgers indicated Hodges had been paid on a particular date, yet there were two requests for payment from the same Hodges. One very tersely worded.

Edwina walked over to the desk and picked up one of the demands from Hodges. "Do you remember a stonemason named Hodges?"

Bascomb shrugged. "I seem to recall a man by that name. Why?"

"He wasn't compensated properly for the work he did in repairing part of the—" She held up a sheet of paper she'd taken from the desk. "—corner on the southwest side. He has written for payment. More than once."

Bascomb came over to the desk, the scent of him and her awareness of his larger form sending a delicious pricking sensation along her arms. "An oversight on Fielding's part? Or one of the others'?"

"The sum was noted paid during Merrywimple's tenure." But Edwina didn't think the handwriting to be his. In fact, she was certain it was not.

"Spindly little nitwit. Looked like a good gust of wind might take him up into the clouds. Nervous disposition." Bascomb stared down at the ledger, a small wrinkle forming between his brows.

"You've said that about all your previous secretaries."

"Untrue. Worthless was stout."

"I meant the nervous disposition. Not their inability to survive a strong breeze." Edwina pursed her lips, which drew her employer's gaze from the ledger to her mouth. That their attraction to each other was mutual was not up for debate. "How long, may I ask, did Merrywimple serve in this position?"

"Mrs. Page would know for sure. He arrived shortly after I inherited. From London."

"Did any of them ever mention finding irregularities in the ledgers that they assumed the previous secretary had made?"

Bascomb quirked a brow. "Well, yes. Larkstub—"

"Larkspur," she corrected him. "You're doing that on purpose."

Bascomb waved a hand, but a tiny smile ghosted his lips. "It doesn't matter. He did mention it to me one morning over breakfast." He paused. "He would only eat boiled eggs for breakfast. Had I known that, I may not have hired him. Imagine, only eating lukewarm, hardened eggs each day."

Edwina had to force her lips into a line to keep from smiling. "Boiled eggs would have been a deterrent to employment?"

"Possibly. At any rate, Larkwith—"

"Larkspur." He was deliberately trying to provoke her, to what end she wasn't sure. Though it was vastly amusing.

"Lark*spur*," he emphasized, "thought Merrywimple had made an error in recording the proper cost of two horses I had Thomas purchase. But I never had a chance to question him further because he resigned a short time later. Said he wouldn't spend another night here no matter how much I paid him."

"And even after such a discussion, did you never seek to review the ledgers yourself? Surely you would find that necessary as often as you change secretaries. Perhaps even personally handle your accounts."

Bascomb's hawkish features froze. Ice dripped from his words as he addressed her. "If I was in charge of the ledgers, there would be no reason to hire a secretary, Collins, now would there?"

"I meant no disrespect, my lord." Her gaze settled on the scar. Bascomb didn't handle the accounts himself because she suspected he *couldn't*. That was the other conclusion she'd reached over the last few days. Southwell, her cousin, had once traveled to Egypt with a man who had taken a blow to the temple during a fight. Though he bore only a small scar on the forehead from the incident, his friend had trouble reading for more than an hour at a time after the fight. He claimed the words would jump about the page and cause his head to ache. Even reading a map presented a problem.

"Do the numbers cause your head to ache, my lord? Since the accident?" Edwina lifted a hand but then lowered it abruptly when he growled.

Bascomb backed away from her, snatched an apple off the tray Meg had left, and went to the window. Taking a savage bite, he ignored her.

Edwina had seen him sketching but not *writing* anything. Given the age of some of his correspondence, it was apparent he hadn't replied to any of it. Had he even *read* any of the letters addressed to him?

"The others never suspected," he said quietly. "Or badgered me." Bascomb shot her a glance filled with anger and a great deal of vulnerability. "I should have tossed you out the moment I saw your skirts dripping mud in my study. You're more trouble than you're worth, Collins."

"It is nothing to be ashamed of, my lord."

"And how would you know, Collins?" He turned toward her, green-gray eyes glowering at her in accusation. "You can't begin to fathom—I can read and write. I'm not some dumb animal."

"My lord, I didn't mean to suggest—" Empathy filled Edwina. Bascomb, beautiful, imposing man that he was, had a weakness. No wonder he was at Rose Abbey and not gracing the balls of London.

"Don't you dare pity me, Collins," he snarled.

"I don't, my lord. In fact, your unpleasant personality makes it fairly easy for me not to."

"You're very insubordinate," he said in a silky tone, eyes narrowed once more on her bosom.

The library grew warmer, much more than could be credited to the meager fire Mrs. Page had lit. Edwina's nipples grew taut beneath his perusal. She turned sharply away.

"Why are you *here*, Collins? At Rose Abbey. And not wed to some tedious gentleman?"

"I don't believe that is relevant to my position." Edwina made her way back to the desk, not caring for his question.

"Oh, it isn't. But I find I am curious about you beyond your exemplary skills, though I'll probably send you back to…where was it?"

He knew perfectly well where she was from. "Hampshire," she murmured.

"Should I expect some rejected suitor to come riding up to the door of Rose Abbey, demanding your return? Or perhaps a cuckolded husband?" There was an odd glint in Bascomb's eyes as he waited for her to answer. A hard edge to his words. A hint of jealousy.

"What makes you think I would cuckold a husband?" Edwina had known Bascomb barely a week, though it felt much longer. As if she'd always known him. The pull in his direction was nearly impossible to resist.

Bascomb strolled over to the desk, discarding the apple core. He stood beside her, so close his breath ruffled her hair. When the tip of his nose dragged along the edge of Edwina's ear, she squeaked in surprise.

"I don't, Collins." One large forefinger brushed against her cheek. "Think you would cuckold a husband. I merely wanted to ascertain if there was such a man."

If Edwina so much as turned, just an inch, her mouth and Bascomb's would touch. This close, she could see that there were striations of gold hovering in his pupils, splintering through the gray-green. She reached up and traced the line of his scar from the corner of his eye to the edge of his mouth.

Bascomb inhaled sharply. "Careful, Collins," he whispered. "This is how Merrywimple was scared off."

"I doubt you would have welcomed the attentions of Merrywimple. Or Worthington. Perhaps Fielding."

He smiled back at her. "Possibly not." He eased away from her. "You should return to your duties."

"Yes. There's much more work to be done."

He snatched several scones off the tea tray before walking out of the library, probably to return to the holes in the roof that seemed to multiply with regularity.

Edwina slumped down into the chair before the desk, disinterested completely in the ledgers before her. Part of her, the wild, reckless version of herself she rarely allowed out, wanted nothing more than to run after Bascomb.

A danger far more frightening than whatever lurked in Rose Abbey.

Chapter Nine

Edwina tossed two of the ledgers along with the small book holding all the notes by Fielding and the others onto her bed. About a quarter of the requests for payment from various tradesmen did not match the notations in the ledgers, too many mistakes to be attributed to merely oversight, especially since the errors had occurred under the watch of each of her predecessors. There was no possible way that *every* secretary Bascomb had hired was that incompetent. Fielding had seen the errors, as had Larkspur, but they'd left Rose Abbey before they could investigate. Bascomb wouldn't see any errors because he was relying on the secretary he hired to do so. And the tenures of those later secretaries had become briefer, the men frightened away from Rose Abbey much sooner.

Before they could put the pieces together?

Picking up a biscuit from the plate she'd set on the pillow, Edwina chewed thoughtfully.

There was a notation in one of the ledgers from over a year ago, in Merrywimple's handwriting. The purchase of a new headstone for the abbess, Lady Renalda. It was a rather large sum. Far more than Edwina would have thought a headstone for a long-dead abbess would have merited. She was sure once she found the receipt for the headstone, *if* she found it, the amount paid wouldn't match the sum in the ledger.

As requested by Mrs. Page, read the note next to the headstone, in Merrywimple's neat handwriting, except it looked like an extra zero had been added to the amount after he'd noted the sum. Edwina squinted. And the seven had subtly been changed to a nine. The ink was a shade darker. Just slightly.

Edwina sat back, tapping her finger against her lips. Had a gravestone actually been purchased? Merrywimple was no longer around for Edwina to ask. Nor could she question Bascomb, who would instantly become defensive about his handicap and lack of attention to the ledgers. And she certainly couldn't ask Mrs. Page.

Tomorrow, Edwina would venture out to the remains of the churchyard and see if there was a grave marker for the abbess. It should be the only piece of stone in the graveyard not cracked or covered with moss, because if indeed it had been purchased, her marker would be much younger than the rest.

A thud sounded outside her door, followed by a soft scratching of fingernails against the wood.

Edwina stared at the door. Fear spiked almost immediately, but she forced it away. Thomas could be lugging about…*something*, though given the hour, that seemed unlikely. Mrs. Page wandering about? No, her quarters were downstairs. Surely it couldn't be Bascomb. Which left only one other option.

Another scratch at the door, much more insistent this time.

"She doesn't like new people."

Edwina refused to be frightened away as Fielding had been, but someone or something was standing outside in the hall. Crawling quietly off the bed, she looked around her room for something to use as a weapon. Grabbing one of her half boots from the floor where she had carelessly tossed her footwear earlier, Edwina took a deep breath and opened the door.

The hall was dark except for a lamp left burning on a table at the top of the stairs. The house itself was silent as a tomb. Quiet. Holding the half boot up, Edwina took a confident step outside her room. "You wanted my attention," she said to the empty hallway. "Now you have it. Show yourself."

A flash of pale cream floated at the very edge of the light cast by the lamp. There came the sound of fingernails scratching along the wall. A vague shape hovered at the end of the hall near the stairs.

"You don't scare me," Edwina said firmly, raising the half boot higher.

The haunting of Rose Abbey was definitely real, but she doubted it was the result of a vengeful spirit. Edwina was willing to bet that when any of Bascomb's secretaries began questioning the discrepancies in the accounts, the "ghost" scared them away. She'd made no secret she was reviewing the ledgers. There was a reason she'd been lured out of her room tonight.

"I'm not leaving," Edwina said into the darkness.

A hand, pale and elongated, seemed to rise from the landing, then it was gone, reappearing a moment later at the foot of the stairs, heading in the direction of the library.

Fine. Edwina was no coward. She would follow this specter.

Emboldened, she strode down the hall to the stairs and descended to the landing. Below her, the house was bathed in nearly complete darkness except for the light of a wall sconce in the foyer. As much as she wanted to race after the departing form, the wisest course would be to go back up the stairs and take the lamp left sitting on the table before descending. She turned and was only mere steps from the lamp when the air stirred the edge of her nightgown, the cotton fluttering around her ankles.

Hands pulled her nightgown, and it tightened around her neck, nearly choking her. She lost her footing on the stairs. The half boot flew from her fingers as she tilted wildly on the step. A cry of alarm left her throat as she fell back, her hip slamming against the wall before she spun toward the landing and the next set of stairs. If she didn't stop herself, Edwina could tumble down further, landing with her neck broken. She grabbed at the banister, her fingers digging into the wood, trying to stop her fall. Her hip banging against the banister, Edwina's head pointed toward the foyer, while her back slammed into the landing.

Edwina held her breath, not daring to look around in the darkness, hoping whoever had tried to pull her down the stairs assumed her to be dead or unconscious.

A lamp flared suddenly in the darkness on the opposite side of the landing. Booted feet, overly large, jumped down the stairs to her.

Panicked, thinking her assassin had returned to finish the job, Edwina rolled away, kicking at the boots with her bare feet.

"Collins." Bascomb's stricken face appeared above her. "Ow. Stop that. It's me. Jonah. Stop." Worry etched the sharp edges of his features as he took hold of her foot doing most of the kicking. "Edwina," he said roughly. "It's me. Jonah."

Edwina stilled. "Your given name is Jonah?"

"Yes. I'm not sure that's what is important at the moment."

He'd gotten to her quickly, far too quickly for someone who should have been asleep in his bed. In her mounting panic, she jerked away from his outstretched hand. "Did you toss me down the stairs?"

His brows drew together. "What? Of course not. Have you hit your head?" Bascomb gently pulled her into a seated position. A warm hand ran down her arm, checking to make sure she was whole. "Where does it hurt?"

"I'm fine—I—" Edwina's voice trembled. She'd nearly broken her neck falling down the stairs. Had she not grabbed at the banister, she might well have tumbled all the way to the floor below.

Someone tried to kill me.

"Edwina," Bascomb rumbled. "You're safe." He reached up to brush a strand of hair out of her eyes. He set down the lamp and pulled her close to the warmth and safety of his bergamot-scented chest. "I have you now. You're safe. I promise."

"I thought—" She allowed herself to be pulled into his embrace.

She curled her hands into his shirt, feeling the firm muscles beneath her fingers. "I heard something in the hall. I—" She stopped herself from telling him about the floating white figure that had lured her out of her room. "I must have tripped." She pulled away from Bascomb. "An accident, nothing more."

The light only reached the lower half of Bascomb's face when he sat back, enough so that she could see him frown. "You accused me of tossing you down the stairs."

"Maybe I did hit my head." She gave him a weak smile and came to her feet.

Mrs. Page appeared in a circle of light below, clutching her robe. "My lord. Miss Collins. What has happened? I heard a thud and a scream." The shadowed light gave her features a stark, menacing look.

Edwina stared down at Mrs. Page, trying to discern whether the housekeeper seemed disappointed not to find her at the base of the stairs in a broken heap.

"I'm sorry you were disturbed, Mrs. Page," Bascomb answered. "Collins couldn't sleep and decided to retrieve a book from the library. Her toe caught on the stair."

Edwina turned to him. "Yes, Mrs. Page. Clumsy of me. My apologies for waking you."

"You should be more careful, Miss Collins," Mrs. Page snipped, grabbing her robe tighter to her thin form before retreating back into the darkness from whence she'd come.

Bascomb got to his feet beside Edwina, his hand sliding down her shoulder to her waist. Holding up the lamp to light the stairs, he waved her forward. "Come, Collins. I'll get you back to your room."

She trembled at his touch, the fear melting away to be replaced with another, more problematic emotion. Edwina was intimately aware that there was little between them except the thin cotton of her nightgown. Her nipples puckered beneath the material as something delicious twisted deep inside her. The top of his shirt was unbuttoned, leaving that tiny space of skin exposed. Edwina couldn't take her eyes off the small triangle, wanting to press her lips to the spot.

Bascomb frowned at her. "Are you sure you haven't hit your head? Because you're staring, Collins. A bit rudely, I might add," he said.

Her hand hovered between them, then she tentatively brushed her fingertips along the line of his jaw before retreating. "You really do have the most beautiful eyes. Seems wasted on a man."

"You did hit your head if you are spouting nonsense like that again." The words were quiet. Soft. He led her up the stairs, arm wrapped firmly around her waist, only stopping when they arrived before the open door of her room.

"I was nearly betrothed. Once." She looked down at her bare feet peeking out from beneath her nightgown. "He was a barrister. Incredibly tedious. He became even more so upon realizing that marriage to me did not include a dowry."

Bascomb inhaled softly. "A great fool, for a barrister." His fingers took her chin, looking down at Edwina. "I was once nearly wed myself. But she didn't care for the scar."

"An even greater fool than my barrister," she whispered. "I find the scar gives you character."

A small grin crossed his lips before his mouth lowered to hers.

Oh.

A soft sound left Edwina at the light pressure. She stood on tiptoe, a wordless plea for him to claim her mouth more fully. Bascomb ran his tongue along the seam of her lips, coaxing her mouth to open beneath his. She darted out her tongue, stroking his, sucking lightly at the tip.

He groaned and pushed Edwina against the wall. Cupping her breast through the thin cotton of her nightgown, he caressed her nipple, teasing and stroking while she pushed herself against him. His hips rocked against hers, the hard length of him pressing between her thighs.

Edwina kissed him harder, her legs parting beneath the onslaught of his bigger body. There was so little between them. Two minuscule layers of clothing. She groaned, rubbing herself against him, feeding the flame burning between them.

He tore his mouth from hers. "I don't believe I'll send you back to Hampshire, Collins." Bascomb pressed his forehead against hers.

"No?" Edwina pressed herself more fully along the muscled length of his body.

"No." He stared down at her, one large blunt finger tracing the line of her jaw. "You are like a peach." A big hand palmed her breast through the nightgown. "You'll be bruised if you are bounced back down to Portsmith."

They stumbled backward into her room, Bascomb kicking the door shut and reaching behind him to throw the lock. She fell through the bed-curtains to the coverlet.

"Ouch." She sat up, pulling out the ledger poking into her side.

"Edwina." He nipped at the skin of her neck before raising his chin to survey the bed. "What is all this?"

"Later." She would tell him all her suspicions later. Her mouth and body pulsed as she lay back on the bed.

"Are you sure, Edwina?" Bascomb started to unbutton his shirt, watching her with hooded eyes. "The impropriety of the situation doesn't escape me."

"I'm not a maid. I—well, there isn't any need to be gentle or spare me the sight of your body."

Oh please, dear God, don't let him spare me.

He tossed his shirt to the floor to reveal a delicious swath of male torso; every muscle carved in exquisite detail rippled as his fingers moved to his trousers. "Damn. My boots." After walking over to a chair, he sat and tugged them off.

"Was it the barrister?" He snapped. "The bloody fool who then didn't want you?"

"Jonah—"

His eyes closed for a moment. "I like the way you say my name. Do it again."

"Jonah," she said in a low, seductive tone. "The barrister doesn't matter."

"No, I don't suppose he does." He unbuttoned his trousers. "I've wanted you since the second you walked into my study. Snarling and spitting like a wet cat. Dripping mud everywhere. Telling me dropping the *a* from your name was an oversight." The trousers were tossed to the floor.

Edwina's eyes widened. She should have guessed, given the size of his feet.

"Did you use up all your bravery earlier, Collins?"

"No." She got up on her knees and reached for him.

Bascomb's mouth fell on hers, hot and possessive, as if he couldn't wait another moment to have her. The heat of his skin singed the tips of her fingers as she traced the lines of his ribs. The curves of his pectorals. The smooth, taut belly.

He fell on her gently, their limbs tangling, the air filling with soft moans and whispers. As he tore at the top of her nightgown, Edwina heard the cotton shredding beneath his assault, then felt the cooler air of the room on her breasts. His thumb rubbed over her nipple, teasing at the peak before he sucked the tip into his mouth.

"Beautiful," he murmured against her breast. "Much lovelier than Fielding."

Edwina started to giggle, but it ended in a moan as his teeth grazed her skin. She pushed her hips up, begging him silently to touch her.

A hand traveled over her thigh before a thick finger traced along her wet slit, gently teasing back and forth, drawing out the wetness.

Edwina gasped as her legs fell apart.

"I think you deserve gentleness, Edwina." Bascomb's mouth left her breast. He kissed the line of her jaw, pausing to brush her lips with his. "Maid or not. But possibly not at this moment." He hissed as her fingers wrapped around the hardness bumping into her thigh. "I want you too much."

She wanted him inside her. Desperately. A part of her, perhaps all of her, wanted to belong to Bascomb. Jonah. It felt right in a way it never had with the barrister. Edwina squeezed. Stroked. Listened to the beautiful sounds he made as she touched him.

He sunk his finger inside her, his thumb brushing lightly over the pulsing bit of flesh hidden in her folds. His fingers moved over her until Edwina lay needy and writhing beneath him.

"Later," he said roughly. "Later I'll worship you properly. Take my time. Feast on every bit of this delicious skin. Possibly for days on end."

Oh, that sounds marvelous. "Yes."

Bascomb flipped her on her stomach, pushing her nightgown up over her thighs, and raised her to her knees. Fingers threaded through her hair. He kissed the line of her neck, tugging down the ends of her nightgown until her shoulders and spine were exposed. The heat of his mouth moved slowly down her spine as she panted beneath him.

A cry left her as Bascomb thrust inside her. He was so much larger than the barrister, which she supposed—

Edwina whimpered as his cock hit a sensitive spot inside her. He hadn't lied. He took her hard. Rough. He moved his hand between her legs with purpose, drawing up her pleasure until she screamed into the pillow.

"I was terrified"—the words came out thick and harsh—"when I found you on the stairs. Never put yourself in such danger again." Bascomb thrust into her so hard her back arched. "My heart stopped, Eddie. I thought I'd lost you and I've only just found you."

Edwina's own heart constricted at the nickname.

Her release was so blinding, so brilliant, the room spun. Bascomb's own climax came a moment later, the warmth of his seed spilling along her thighs. His mouth fell to the back of her neck. Beautiful words fell from his lips. Gorgeous, wicked things.

Bascomb rolled to the side, taking her with him. His arms pulled her close. "Did I hurt you?"

"Only in the best way."

His arms tightened. They lay quietly together listening to the fire in the hearth. "It looks like rain tomorrow," he murmured, pressing a kiss to her cheek.

Edwina laced her fingers with his and squeezed.

CHAPTER TEN

EDWINA FLIPPED OPEN the ledgers once more, wiggling on her chair at the soreness between her thighs. They'd parted quietly as pearl-gray light filled her room. Kissing her hard, Bascomb had whispered he would see her at breakfast, his big hand trailing down her body as if reluctant to leave her.

But Edwina hadn't awoken until nearly nine o'clock, flustered and rubbing the sleep from her eyes. Bascomb had already been gone when she'd reached the breakfast room, which was probably just as well. She wasn't certain how to approach him after last night. Yes, he wanted her to stay, but in what capacity? Would they return to their slightly contentious, flirtatious relationship? Or would there be something more?

Frowning, she took in the still-thunderous skies outside the library window. The sun hadn't yet decided to make an appearance at Rose Abbey. Mist hovered just above the grass as she looked out over the ruins of the abbey. Her eyes landed on the church, and she remembered her decision to search for the grave of the abbess.

"Good morning, Miss Collins." Mrs. Page came through the doors, a tray in her hands. "I thought you might like tea and a bite of something to eat. You didn't come down for breakfast."

"No, I fear after my near tumble down the stairs"—she watched the housekeeper for any reaction—"I found myself tossing and turning." A blush stole across her cheeks as she thought of her and

Bascomb entangled on her bed. "I overslept."

A sound came from the housekeeper. Disappointment at not succeeding in pushing Edwina down the stairs? She tried to discern Mrs. Page's mood and failed. Accusing the housekeeper outright of trying to throw her down the stairs and dressing as a ghost would gain her nothing. Edwina would need proof to convince Bascomb that Mrs. Page was behind the haunting and skimming money from his accounts.

"An unfortunate occurrence, Miss Collins. You nearly broke your neck last night. I leave a lamp burning at the end of the hall for a reason—namely, for you to use."

There wasn't anyone else at Rose Abbey capable of manipulating the ledgers besides Mrs. Page. Or dressing up like a ghost. Mrs. Oates, the cook, never left the kitchens and was half-blind. Mr. Oates was seventy if he was a day and possessed a terrible limp. Meg, sweet and fragile, was far too timid. Thomas, though kind, was a simpleton.

That left Mrs. Page. But the question remained. *Why* would Mrs. Page do such a thing?

"I appreciate the tray, Mrs. Page." Edwina poured herself a cup of tea. "You've been here a long time, haven't you? At Rose Abbey." Perhaps if she engaged the older woman in polite conversation, Mrs. Page might inadvertently reveal something.

"All my life." The housekeeper clasped her hands and looked up at the portrait of the abbess. "I was born here. You could say I grew up with Lady Renalda."

What an odd and slightly morbid way to put things. "So you believe the abbey is haunted by Lady Renalda's vengeful spirit?"

"Wouldn't you find yourself vengeful, Miss Collins, if you were not only evicted from your home but also murdered in it? For gold? A title?" Mrs. Page raised a brow. "Add to it having your name and reputation sullied?" The housekeeper stepped up to the fireplace. "I'm sure McDeaver"—her lip curled slightly—"told you the entire tale. He seems to delight in informing Lord Bascomb's secretaries of the gruesome history of Rose Abbey. What a collection of weak gentlemen. Afraid of their own shadows. London must be filled with milksops. Merrywimple in particular behaved as if there were monsters hiding beneath the bed."

"But you aren't frightened."

"No." The housekeeper pierced her with a sharp look. "I've nothing to fear from Lady Renalda."

"So you've seen her ghost, then?" Edwina leaned forward, searching the woman for any tic or tell that would give her away.

"I feel her presence. The scent of roses that always accompanies her. Lady Renalda was a brave, courageous woman who deserved far better than to be reduced to a ghost story meant to frighten children."

The housekeeper defended the abbess quite fiercely.

"Lady Renalda," Mrs. Page continued in a crisp tone, "was my ancestor. A cousin, if you wish to think of her as such, many times removed. I am protective of her memory and Rose Abbey, as my mother was and her mother before her. My family has served the constant stream of Lord Bascombs for many years. Rose Abbey is my home."

Her sense that the housekeeper was possessive of the estate hadn't been in error. Rose Abbey belonged to Mrs. Page's family as much as it did Lord Bascomb, considering how long her family had been here.

"When the first Lord Bascomb came to evict the nuns from Rose Abbey—"

"They knew each other, Lady Renalda and that first Lord Bascomb," Mrs. Page interrupted. "Something I'm sure McDeaver leaves out of his tale. Far easier to paint her as a somewhat mad, greedy woman who merely refused to get out of the way." Mrs. Page shook her head. "Lady Renalda rejected Alfred Duston's proposal of marriage and instead chose to serve the church." She glanced at Edwina. "That was the name of the first Lord Bascomb. Alfred Duston. He jumped at the opportunity to become a titled lord and evict the woman who'd once rejected him. Duston's sword took her life. In this very room.

Can you imagine? A woman you had once loved. All because your pride and greed dictated you do so."

"No." The entire story made Edwina slightly ill. Poor Lady Renalda.

"Alfred Duston left a journal of sorts. More a warning to those who would succeed him. I think it must be in His Lordship's study, though I doubt he's read it." Her eyes caught Edwina's.

She knows he likely cannot.

"Duston got his title but was haunted by the horror of his actions for the remainder of his days. He wandered about Rose Abbey, even after he married, speaking to Lady Renalda. Begging forgiveness for what he'd done to her and her nuns."

"But not *all* her nuns."

"No," Mrs. Page said quietly. "Only a handful. The rest escaped. Perhaps they took the treasure of Rose Abbey with them or hid it. Because Duston never found the gold plate and jewels the abbey supposedly possessed. The Crown wasn't pleased with his failure. His stature in London faded as a result, despite the title." She shot Edwina a thin, smug smile. "No Bascomb has been happy here since."

"Not even the previous one?" Bascomb had inferred to Edwina that the housekeeper and his uncle had had a long-standing affair.

Mrs. Page's cheeks colored. "I've duties to attend to, Miss Collins. Now that the roads are clear, I have errands in Portsmith. Please excuse me." She nodded to Edwina, brushed past her with a sweep of her agitated skirts, and sailed out the door.

Edwina stared at the doorway for the longest time, convinced now she had a reason for the doctored accounts, the multitude of repairs, and the mysterious ghost that haunted Rose Abbey.

Mrs. Page requests a new gravestone for the abbess.

She stood and went over to the fireplace, the deep well of sorrow that seemed to hang over the estate finally making sense.

"I'm sorry," she whispered to the portrait of Lady Renalda. "I'm so very sorry."

Chapter Eleven

Edwina worked for several more hours after the departure of Mrs. Page, carefully delving back into the notes of Merrywimple, Larkspur, and Worthington. The theft from Bascomb's accounts had been occurring in a steady trickle since he'd inherited the estate eighteen months ago. It was really very clever. A lord who couldn't review his own accounts. A series of secretaries who would be scared off if they got too close to the truth. If she hadn't arrived, the theft could have continued for years before Bascomb realized what was happening.

Speaking of which, her employer had yet to make an appearance in the library as was his habit. Edwina tried not to be disappointed. It was only last night—

"Excuse me, miss. I've brought you a fresh pot of tea."

Edwina startled at the sound of Meg's voice, grateful the maid had interrupted the direction of her thoughts. Leaving the desk, she stretched her arms overhead and made her way to the settee. "Thank you. The pot Mrs. Page brought me earlier has grown quite cold."

As before, Meg set down the tray but kept her gaze on the portrait of Lady Renalda. The maid sidled along the wall to approach the desk and pick up Edwina's now cold pot of tea. The girl glanced at Edwina. "You aren't scared like them, are you, Miss Collins?"

"You mean the other secretaries?" Edwina bit into a biscuit. "No, I am not." She wasn't about to allow Mrs. Page strutting about in a white sheet to scare her away from discovering the extent of the theft from Lord Bascomb. Nor would she allow Mrs. Page to get away with her assault of Edwina the previous night.

She tapped her lips with a finger. Mrs. Page must have run down the stairs after Edwina had fallen, discarded the sheet or whatever it was she wore when she pretended to be the ghost, then appeared below in her robe, acting as if she'd just been awakened.

"Mr. Fielding told me he saw lights in the graveyard and the church." Meg gave her a wide-eyed look. "Bobbing about in the darkness. Scared him something terrible. Have you ever seen lights, Miss Collins?"

"No. And I don't believe in ghosts. You shouldn't either, Meg."

The maid glanced over at Edwina's desk stacked with papers and the ledgers. "Should I bring you another pot in a little while? Since you'll be working on the ledgers?"

"No, actually I think I'm done for the day. Now that the rain has passed, I believe I'll walk about the grounds and explore the ruins. The architecture is quite lovely. Possibly take a look at the gravestones or peek inside the church. Lord Bascomb is bound to come looking for me, and Mrs. Page has gone to Portsmith. Will you please inform him of my whereabouts?"

"Yes, but—Mrs. Page says for us—the staff, I mean—not to get close to the churchyard." Meg bit her lip. "Best be careful, Miss Collins. The graves are loose at the edge of the cliff. And—" The girl's eyes shifted to the portrait of the abbess. "Well, and *she* doesn't like it when you wander about and get close to her nuns." Meg lowered her voice to a whisper. "The ones in the ground, I mean."

"Have you seen her, Meg? The abbess?"

The maid's feet shifted, fingers plucking at the fabric. "Only once, miss. All in white. Skirts floating about. I heard something scratching at my window, and when I looked outside—" The girl paled. "I was scared something terrible. I heard how they talked about Rose Abbey in Portsmith…but never believed it." She shook her head. "But there ain't many opportunities in the village. Wages here are more than I can earn at the tavern or taking in mending." Her thin shoulders gave a shrug. "Been here since Lord Bascomb came. I mean, *this* Lord Bascomb, miss."

"And you're the only maid that's ever worked here?"

"Another one of the girls in Portsmith came with me, but she left. Now it's just me and Thomas. And Mrs. Page told me there's nothing to fear from Lady Renalda."

"There isn't," Edwina said firmly. "If anything, say a prayer for Lady Renalda and her nuns."

Chapter Twelve

Edwina pulled her shawl tighter around her shoulders and strolled through the remains of the abbey, admiring the architecture of the wide, gothic arches. The ground here was swampy in patches, moisture still dripping down the stone. She jumped across a string of puddles, intent on making her way to the churchyard. The wind kicked up, billowing her skirts as she approached the first grave marker. She took her time, peering down in an attempt to read the stone etched with dates, but the elements had erased the names from most of the stones.

Not only did she not find the grave of Lady Renalda, but none of the stones appeared to have been recently carved.

A heavy weight landed firmly on Edwina's shoulders at the news she must give Bascomb.

He'd become important to her in such a short time, almost from the instant Edwina had caught sight of him, insulting her from behind the desk in his study. And regardless of what their future held after their passionate encounter last night, Edwina owed it to Bascomb to tell him that his housekeeper was skimming from his accounts and had frightened away the other secretaries from Rose Abbey.

Not to mention that she had tried to harm Edwina.

She stepped over a small, nearly dead rosebush, pulling up her skirts, and felt something in her pocket. Reaching inside, she pulled out the leaf she'd found beneath the desk. Edwina studied the leaf, now dry and starting to crumble. When she returned to the library today, she would look more closely at the bookcases along the wall. Now that she knew more of the story of Lady Renalda, Edwina hadn't any doubt that there was a hidden door. The other nuns would have gathered in her office when the soldiers came.

If the abbey possessed any wealth, it was reasonable to expect that the gold went with the remainder of her flock, all without being seen by the soldiers. Which meant there was a passageway out of Rose Abbey, accessible through the library.

And someone was using it. To throw books at teapots and topple over bookcases. To terrify Bascomb's legion of secretaries.

The ground shifted beneath her feet, and she looked up, surprised to find herself at the very edge of the churchyard where the cliffs began. The sea stretched out before her, still rough and roiling from the recent storm. The tang of salt filled the air. Edwina turned and faced the ruins and the stone portion of the older part of Rose Abbey that had once been Lady Renalda's residence, noting the odd way the rosebushes had been planted as they came toward the church.

She cocked her head.

The bushes weren't planted in the pattern of any garden Edwina had ever enjoyed. There were no gatherings for a bench or a place of prayer. Nothing at all like the roses closer to the abbey and main house.

Incredibly odd.

Looking down over the cliffs, careful not to get too close, she realized a rosebush had been planted by itself a few feet from her. Then another, leading around a cluster of graves to the church.

She walked back and forth several times, becoming surer with every step. The rosebushes were markers, planted on the lawn in such a way with purpose. Like a map to buried treasure.

Or a series of tunnels.

Lady Renalda hadn't inhabited Rose Abbey for nearly three hundred years, and no rosebush, no matter how determined, could live that long without help. Someone was ensuring the line of rosebushes stayed intact. Perhaps a series of housekeepers.

Edwina took off in the direction of the church. She jumped over one of the sinking graves and onto the crumbling steps of the church, her heart beating wildly at her discovery. A door in the library was an entry point from Lady Renalda's office to a series of tunnels. The church seemed a likely spot for at least one exit. If the abbess had indeed bought time for her flock to escape, some of them might have come to the church and stripped it of whatever gold and jeweled relics it possessed, then gone back into the tunnel. The soldiers would never have seen them.

Tentatively she tiptoed inside, nose wrinkling at the scents of mildew and dust. Broken stone lay in heaps along the floor. Weeds grew through every crack. The entire space spoke of age and disuse.

Except for the muddy footprints coming from behind the altar.

Edwina's heart nearly stopped in her chest. She wasn't the only one who had ventured here. Meg had mentioned lights in the church at night. So had at least one of Bascomb's former secretaries.

She climbed over a large stack of bricks following the muddy trail, cursing when her skirts caught on, of all things, a bloody rosebush that had found its way inside, springing through a crack in the floor. When she reached down to pull her skirt free, she saw it.

A latch. In the floor.

Stumbling over the debris in the church, she made her way over to a trapdoor set into the base of the altar. The muddy footprints led right to the edge.

I knew it.

The door must lead to a tunnel. Was Mrs. Page using the tunnel to come to the church at night and look for the abbey's hidden gold? And she must also be using the passage to spy on Bascomb's secretaries, scaring them away when she saw them getting too close to the truth.

Edwina thought of the sounds she had heard in the library. The bookcase that had nearly crushed her. The stupid leaf.

She had to tell Bascomb.

Kneeling, Edwina lifted open the small trapdoor cut into the stone floor, the hinges making not a sound. Someone had recently oiled them, no doubt. Peering into the darkness of the tunnel, she could make out nothing. A candle or lamp was needed.

Drat.

Just as Edwina resolved to return to the house and retrieve a light, a shuffle sounded behind her.

And then the world went black.

>>>><<<<

EDWINA BLINKED IN the darkness, wincing as she tried to raise her head. She was sprawled on her back in the dirt. Silence surrounded her. Carefully, she sat up, her fingers touching the tender spot at the back of her head. The last thing she remembered was peering into the hole beneath the altar and thinking she needed light to properly explore the tunnel below. How long had she been lying here?

A sudden rush of panic flooded Edwina. There wasn't so much as a pinprick of light. She reached up with both her hands and touched nothing but emptiness. The trapdoor must be above her, but there was no way to reach it, not without a ladder or a rope.

She took in a shaky breath, trying to calm her wildly beating heart. Someone would come looking for her. Eventually. Meg knew she was walking to the church. When Edwina didn't arrive for tea, Meg would inform Bascomb.

Edwina calmed herself. Bascomb would look for her. He would. She only had to stay put for a time.

Whoever had hit Edwina, and it could only be Mrs. Page, had pushed her into the hole. The housekeeper knew her secret had been discovered. She might return at any moment and do far worse than merely hit Edwina over the head. Desperate people did desperate things. Going to Portsmith for the day was merely a ruse.

Edwina tried to get her bearings and found it impossible in the darkness. The tunnel undoubtedly led to the library, but there wasn't any telling where else. She could just as easily find herself on the beach or lost in the woods outside of Rose Abbey. But any alternative was better than simply waiting for Mrs. Page to return and finish her off.

Wishing fervently for a candle as the thick blackness enveloped her, Edwina stretched out her arms to either side. The tunnel didn't seem to be too wide. Her fingertips touched the rough edges of stone. Definitely man-made. Edwina walked carefully in a circle, one hand on the wall, until her fingers curved away into more emptiness. The tunnel. Drifting her fingers in the air, she met stone again.

Very good. Only one tunnel out.

Carefully, she inched through the passage, her fingers trailing along the stone on either side. How long had it taken someone to build this tunnel? It must have been created around the same time the abbey had been built.

After a few moments, her right hand touched only emptiness as the wall fell away.

Damn.

She'd been afraid of this. Feeling her way around, Edwina could tell that the tunnel split. Walking to her right a few steps, she was assaulted by the scents of salt and damp earth. The distant rumble of waves met her ears. Edwina ignored the small burst of triumph that she'd been right. The nuns had fled to the beach. The knowledge didn't help her at the moment.

"Not that way," she whispered, turning back the way she'd come. She felt her way to the original passage and moved forward.

Her half boots scuffed along the dirt as she continued on, hoping she would end up at the library. After about half an hour, the tunnel seemed to take a slight incline. The toe of her boot hit something solid.

The bottom of stairs.

Holding on to the wall, she felt her way upward until the pitch-black of the tunnel lightened enough so she could see her hand in front of her face. A door was in front of her. She could see the outline. Reaching the top of the stairs, she ran her fingers over the wall, feeling for a lever or trigger to open the hidden door. Finally, her thumb caught on something.

The door, actually the lower part of the bookcase, swung open with a swoosh.

Edwina recognized that sound. She'd heard it before. Just before a book was thrown at her pot of tea.

I knew it wasn't a bloody ghost.

Stepping into the library, Edwina watched as the door slid smoothly back into place. A book, covered in burgundy leather, had fallen forward but now snapped back into place as the door shut.

The lever to open the door.

Examining the bookcase, Edwina searched for the outline of the door and couldn't see it. Impossible to find if one wasn't looking. How had Fielding seen it?

"Collins." Bascomb was seated at her desk, staring at her. His features were creased with relief. "Thank God. Collins."

Edwina pointed at the bookcase. "There is a—"

"What the bloody hell are you doing in the wall?" he interrupted, running a hand through his hair. "I've been searching for you for hours. No one in Portsmith has seen you, and I—" He came forward in a rush and took her in his arms, kissing her cheek, her forehead, and finally her mouth.

Oh. He's been worried.

Her knees buckled, but Bascomb held her tight. Squeezing her until she gasped for air. "Jonah. I can't breathe."

He cupped the back of her head, the gray-green of his eyes luminous in the dim light of the room. "I couldn't find you. I thought—"

"Ouch." Edwina winced as his fingers found the lump at the base of her skull.

Bascomb immediately pulled his fingers away, dark with blood. "You're bleeding."

"I am?"

He pulled her onto his lap.

Edwina struggled. Half-heartedly. "I'm fine. Set me down. Someone might see."

"I don't care." Pulling a handkerchief from his pocket, he pressed the cloth to her head gently, rocking her as if she was a child.

"I'm quite well, Jonah. I have to tell you—"

"I thought you left Rose Abbey," Bascomb whispered. "I went to Portsmith and looked. Searched. I found Mrs. Page at the butcher shop. She hadn't seen you either." A stricken look flashed across his features. "I thought you were gone. Because of last night."

"Oh." She kissed the line of his jaw. Edwina stroked his cheek until the muscles in his arms relaxed. Bascomb, big and vital. Strong. Blustering about like a bull. A woman had left him. He'd alluded to it last night. She made a mental note to return to that topic later. "No." Her lips brushed his. "Never."

"You *said* you were leaving. Didn't even leave me a note. Not that I could have read it. At least not well."

"Jonah, I didn't leave. Clearly. You watched me walk out of a secret door in the library. I was in a tunnel, and—wait, who told you I left Rose Abbey? Let me guess, Mrs. Page, I'll warrant."

Bascomb's brow wrinkled in confusion. "No. Page was in Portsmith. Buying a roast. Meg came to me wringing her hands. She said when she brought you tea, you stomped about, hands in the air. You couldn't take the isolation. She said that I could send your things. Thomas said you didn't even wait to have your trunk brought down but insisted you be taken to Portsmith immediately to catch the first coach to London. So I went to Portsmith."

"Is that what he told you?" Edwina looked into his beautiful gray-green eyes. "But I'm not from London, as I've reminded you often enough. Hampshire, my lord." The revelation of who was truly behind the manipulation of the ledgers and the haunting had Edwina's head swimming. It had *never* been Mrs. Page.

"Thomas is simple. London is the only city he likely can name outside of Portsmith." Bascomb pulled her to him, pressing the tip of his nose into her neck. "Eddie. What the bloody hell were you doing in the wall? You smell of dirt. You're bleeding. Covered in cobwebs."

Edwina sat back, tossing the handkerchief on the table. "Thomas isn't simple. Meg isn't timid. They've been stealing from you since you came to Rose Abbey. There is no ghost. It's Meg, dressed up and fluttering about. Thomas pushed over the bookcase."

"Dear God. The blow to your head addled you. Meg?"

"There are mistakes in the ledgers. Small, tiny little oversights. Tradesmen marked as paid, but not truly paid. Numbers altered. They knew you didn't check the ledgers. The sum they've taken is quite large all added together. Hundreds of pounds. When your secretaries discovered the irregularities, they were frightened away before making their suspicions known."

Bascomb sat back, shaking his head. "That's impossible. It can't be true."

"Entirely true, I'm afraid." Thomas came into the library, pushing Mrs. Page before him, a pistol in her back. "Do I look simple to you now, my lord?"

"Thomas." Bascomb stood.

"Surprised?" He pushed Mrs. Page away from him and pointed the gun at Bascomb. "One move and I'll blow your head off, my lord."

Bascomb's hands curled into fists. His eyes narrowed. "You bastard. You stole from me."

"Well, you can't check your own ledgers. I'm really not to blame for your lack of attention. Or is it intelligence? I'm not the simpleton in the room."

A growl came from Bascomb. The scar stood out stark against his cheek. "I'll see you hang for this."

Edwina placed a hand on his arm, terrified Thomas would shoot him.

"Doubtful. If Miss Collins had just stayed in the tunnel or died in any of the other attempts we made to rid Rose Abbey of her presence, you might have ended up with nothing more than bruised pride at knowing you'd been fleeced." Thomas shrugged. "As it is, I suppose you'll all be going into the tunnels together." He looked at Edwina. "You've more lives than a cat, Miss Collins. I'm not sure how you escaped the bookcase. Or Meg pushing you down the stairs."

"Agility," Edwina snapped.

Meg strolled into the room, looking nothing like the timid little maid Edwina had taken her to be. Dressed in a gown of green silk, hair carefully coiled with a small hat atop, Meg looked askance at Thomas. "She survived." Meg's eye roved over Edwina. "Unbelievable. Well, I suppose we'll have to shoot them all. Just to be sure. No one will find the bodies in the tunnel. Maybe they'll think the ghost—" She giggled and waved a hand at Lady Renalda. "—did away with them. Now"— her mouth hardened—"my lord, if you will please tell us where the gold is, we'll shoot you first and you won't have to see what Thomas does to Miss Collins."

"There isn't any gold," Bascomb snarled. "There never was. And even if I did know the location, I wouldn't tell you."

Mrs. Page looked down at the rug.

She knows where the gold is.

"A pity. I suppose you need an inducement. I refuse to believe your uncle didn't leave you at least a clue." Meg glared at him and tugged on a pair of gloves. "But perhaps he told his lover. Thomas, shoot Mrs. Page if she doesn't tell us this instant"—Meg's voice rose an octave—"where it is."

Mrs. Page raised her chin. "Go ahead, Meg. You deceitful thing. Lady Renalda didn't give up Rose Abbey's secrets, and neither will I."

"Fine. We'll do this the hard way." She nodded to Thomas to point the pistol at Edwina.

Edwina watched Thomas raise the pistol. Mrs. Page screamed, and Bascomb roared as he launched himself at Thomas. The air in the library became thick, suddenly, with the cloying scent of roses. A wall of air shoved Edwina to the floor so hard her forehead hit the rug. She turned her head to see Meg, screaming in terror and running for the doors.

And those heavy, thick doors fell completely off their hinges, knocking Meg to the floor.

A sound of pure fury filled the room. Like a hurricane forming inside the library.

Lady Renalda's portrait sailed across the room, the corner of the heavy gilt frame catching Thomas in the eye. Rose petals fluttered in the air. Clutching his bleeding eye, Thomas wailed in pain, dropping the gun. The weapon skittered across the floor, spinning to land right in front of Edwina's nose.

Edwina lay gasping. Stunned. Roses permeated the very air around her. The press of a hand gently stroked the back of her head, though no one else was anywhere near her. Peace filled her. Calm. Stretching out her hand, Edwina curled her fingers around the gun, though it was hardly necessary. Meg was moaning in pain. Blood streamed from Thomas's eye.

Mrs. Page was on her knees, weeping, a rose petal clutched against her chest.

Bascomb shot Edwina a stunned look, his shocked gaze landing on the floor where the portrait of Lady Renalda rested.

"Lady Renalda," Edwina whispered as a tear ran down her cheek. "I'm so sorry I said I didn't believe in you."

Epilogue

Six months later

R OSE ABBEY *WAS* haunted.

Edwina walked to the edge of the graveyard, now neatly fenced off as it should have been years ago. The ruins of the church and what remained of the abbey would continue to stand until they crumbled back into the earth. Neither Bascomb nor Edwina had the heart to take either from Lady Renalda. She'd already lost so much.

"Thank you," Mrs. Page said from beside Edwina, looking at the largest stone in the graveyard. It wasn't easy to miss. Stark and white, it bore an angel carved atop, and one of Rose Abbey's bloodred rosebushes was already curling about the stone. Mrs. Page's doing, no doubt.

"It was the very least Jonah and I could do. I still think it impossible. What happened that day. But I've no other way to explain any of it." Edwina had tried. One explanation was that a gust of wind had blown Lady Renalda's portrait from the wall, except the windows had been shut. Another was that the doors hadn't been properly maintained so the hinges had failed. Also not the case.

"So"—the housekeeper gave her a sideways glance—"you still don't believe in ghosts?"

Edwina thought of all the times in the last few months when a comforting presence had enveloped her and she'd smelled roses in the air. The day she and Jonah had married, red rose petals had scattered across the bed. "No, but I believe in Lady Renalda."

"I think she's at peace now," Mrs. Page said. "She is loved here. Finally. As she always should have been. I should tell you, Lady Bascomb. I know where—"

Taking the housekeeper's hand, Edwina stopped Mrs. Page from finishing. "We don't want to know. Keep Rose Abbey's secrets, Mrs. Page, as your mother and grandmother did. As far as Lord Bascomb is concerned, there is no gold buried away beneath the rosebushes." Only a series of tunnels, the responsibility of maintaining the rosebushes used as a map falling to each housekeeper of Rose Abbey. The secret passed down through the generations.

Her husband had chosen to keep the passage open only to the beach, sealing the entrance from the church due to safety concerns. *"You never know,"* he'd said and winked at Edwina, *"when we'll need to escape a Viking raid."*

"I blame myself for Meg. And Thomas. You should dismiss me."

"I'm not going to endure Lord Bascomb alone, Mrs. Page." Edwina squeezed her fingers again. Page had a hard, crusty shell, but inside beat a generous heart. She could not have known that the two servants were actually husband and wife. They'd fled London after stealing from their last employer and ended up in Portsmith. Hearing the tales of hidden gold at Rose Abbey from the tavern owner's wife, the pair had sought positions at Rose Abbey. It was Meg who'd ascertained Bascomb's handicap shortly after Merrywimple had arrived.

"It was kind of you to spare them. They didn't deserve it."

"I'm not sure they'd agree. But indentured servitude halfway across the world isn't nooses around their necks." Meg and Thomas should have been hanged, but Edwina had asked for them to be exiled instead. Even though they'd tried to kill her. More than once. But she thought Lady Renalda would have preferred leniency.

The first thing Edwina had done once the constable had been

called was make sure the portrait of the abbess was returned to its proper place in the library. She still worked at the same desk, pausing throughout the day to speak to Lady Renalda. Edwina was fairly certain she listened.

"I should go back, Mrs. Page." She placed a hand on the housekeeper's shoulder, silently saying another prayer of thanks to Lady Renalda and her brave nuns. "Stay as long as you like. I'll check on Mrs. Oates and dinner."

The End

About the Author

Kathleen Ayers is the bestselling author of steamy Regency and Victorian romance. She's been a hopeful romantic and romance reader since buying Sweet Savage Love at a garage sale when she was fourteen while her mother was busy looking at antique animal planters. She has a weakness for tortured, witty alpha males who can't help falling for intelligent, sassy heroines.

A Texas transplant (from Pennsylvania) Kathleen spends most of her summers attempting to grow tomatoes (a wasted effort) and floating in her backyard pool with her two dogs, husband and son. When not writing she likes to visit her "happy place" (Newport, RI.), wine bars, make homemade pizza on the grill, and perfect her charcuterie board skills. Visit her at www.kathleenayers.com.

Printed in Great Britain
by Amazon

MISS EDWINA COLLINS, IMPOVERISHED SPINSTER, HAS NO CHOICE BUT TO SEEK EMPLOYMENT AFTER THE DEATH OF HER FATHER..

Stubbornly refusing to take charity from her cousin, Lord Southwell, she applies for the position of secretary at Rose Abbey, a remote estate rumored to be haunted. Edwina doesn't believe in ghosts; despite the horrible tales she hears. Or the number of secretaries that have fled the position before her.

Lord Bascomb has lost a half-dozen secretaries, all too terrified to remain at Rose Abbey. On the recommendation of Lord Southwell, he offers the position to "Edwin" Collins, only to find Edwina Collins on his doorstep instead.

Soon, Edwina has more to worry over than tales of a ghost. She and Bascomb are unexpectedly, fiercely, attracted to each other.

And someone or something doesn't want Edwina at Rose Abbey.

WWW.DRAGONBLADEPUBLISHING.COM

ISBN 9798864325452